LI'L RIP HAYWIRE

ADVENTURES

Escape from Camp Cooties

LI'L RIP HAYWIRE

ADVENTURES
Escape from Camp Cooties

DAN THOMPSON

Andrews McMeel
Publishing®

a division of Andrews McMeel Universal

MISSION JOURNAL, DAY ONE. SOMEWHERE IN THE JUNGLE OF TANGO BOOM BANGO.

You might think it's crazy that I'm writing in a journal while trekking through a mosquito infested, squishy jungle. Or maybe you're wondering what a twelve-year-old kid would even be doing in such a lethally sticky place.

But I'm no ordinary kid; my name is Rip Haywire and I'm a soldier of fortune. That means I spend most of my time hunting for the hidden treasure of lost civilizations. It beats school, right?

And that's the reason why I have to write in this stupid journal. Since I don't go to school, my dad thinks I need to do something to exercise my mind, as if finding lost treasure was a piece of cake.

But my dad says all adventurers need to know how to write, and if I want to get a machete for Christmas, I better get cracking. And, boy, do I want that machete for Christmas. Hacking jungle vines with a Junior Scout knife is the pits.

OK, OK, maybe my dad is the real soldier of fortune and he brings me along because he can't afford day care.

But I've grown to become an indispensable part of Dad's missions, thanks to his training. Once I learned to walk, it got a lot easier.

After that, I learned how to disarm booby traps. Dad said my small hands are good for this task.

My dad is the best adventurer ever. He's got all the qualities that you need to be an awesome soldier of fortune.

AWESOME SOLDIER OF FORTUNE GUIDE

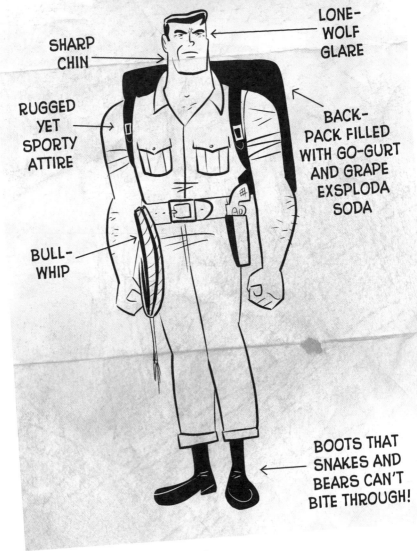

SHARP CHIN

LONE-WOLF GLARE

RUGGED YET SPORTY ATTIRE

BACK-PACK FILLED WITH GO-GURT AND GRAPE EXSPLODA SODA

BULL-WHIP

BOOTS THAT SNAKES AND BEARS CAN'T BITE THROUGH!

Today Dad sent me out on a solo mission to hunt down the lost gem of Tango Boom Bango. Why people go nuts about lost gems, I'll never know. I'd trade a lost gem for a lost rocket launcher any day. But it's my first solo mission and if you ask me, it's about time.

Not to brag, but I've been pretty handy to have around on adventures. Like this one time when Dad and I were out on a top secret mission . . .

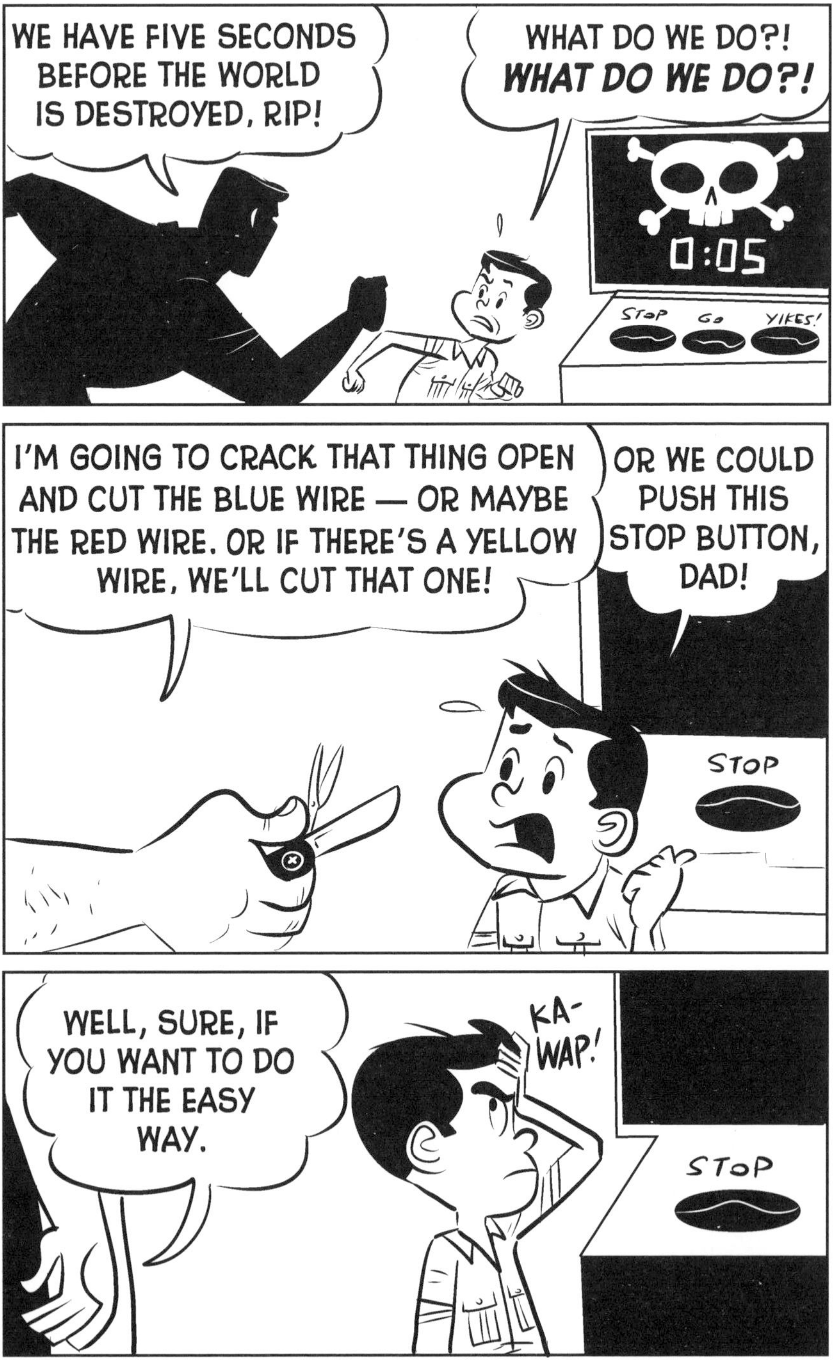
WE HAVE FIVE SECONDS BEFORE THE WORLD IS DESTROYED, RIP!
WHAT DO WE DO?! *WHAT DO WE DO?!*
0:05
STOP
GO
YIKES!
I'M GOING TO CRACK THAT THING OPEN AND CUT THE BLUE WIRE — OR MAYBE THE RED WIRE. OR IF THERE'S A YELLOW WIRE, WE'LL CUT THAT ONE!
OR WE COULD PUSH THIS STOP BUTTON, DAD!
STOP
WELL, SURE, IF YOU WANT TO DO IT THE EASY WAY.
KA-WAP!
STOP

You're probably wondering why you haven't heard about the kid who saved the world from being turned into flaming chunks. It's because the mission never occurred . . . officially.

But it totally happened.

Oh, by the way, do me a favor and don't tell anybody I told you.

Life as a junior soldier of fortune can be lonely without a sidekick. This is my puppy, TNT. I named him that because I figured he would have an explosive attitude. Boy, was I wrong.

Here he is ordering pizza during an adventure:

Anyway, TNT can come in handy. Today, he helped me get away with that gem!

The Doofus Brothers are the stupidest, ugliest, and smelliest mercenaries around.

They're so stupid that I bet they even get their own names mixed up . . .

So ugly that mirrors refuse to cast their reflections . . .

So smelly that skunks think they're related to them.

But I will say this about the Doofus Brothers: no matter how stupid, ugly, and smelly they are, they always seem to get in my way just as I'm about to do something that would get me the trophy for best junior soldier of fortune of all time!

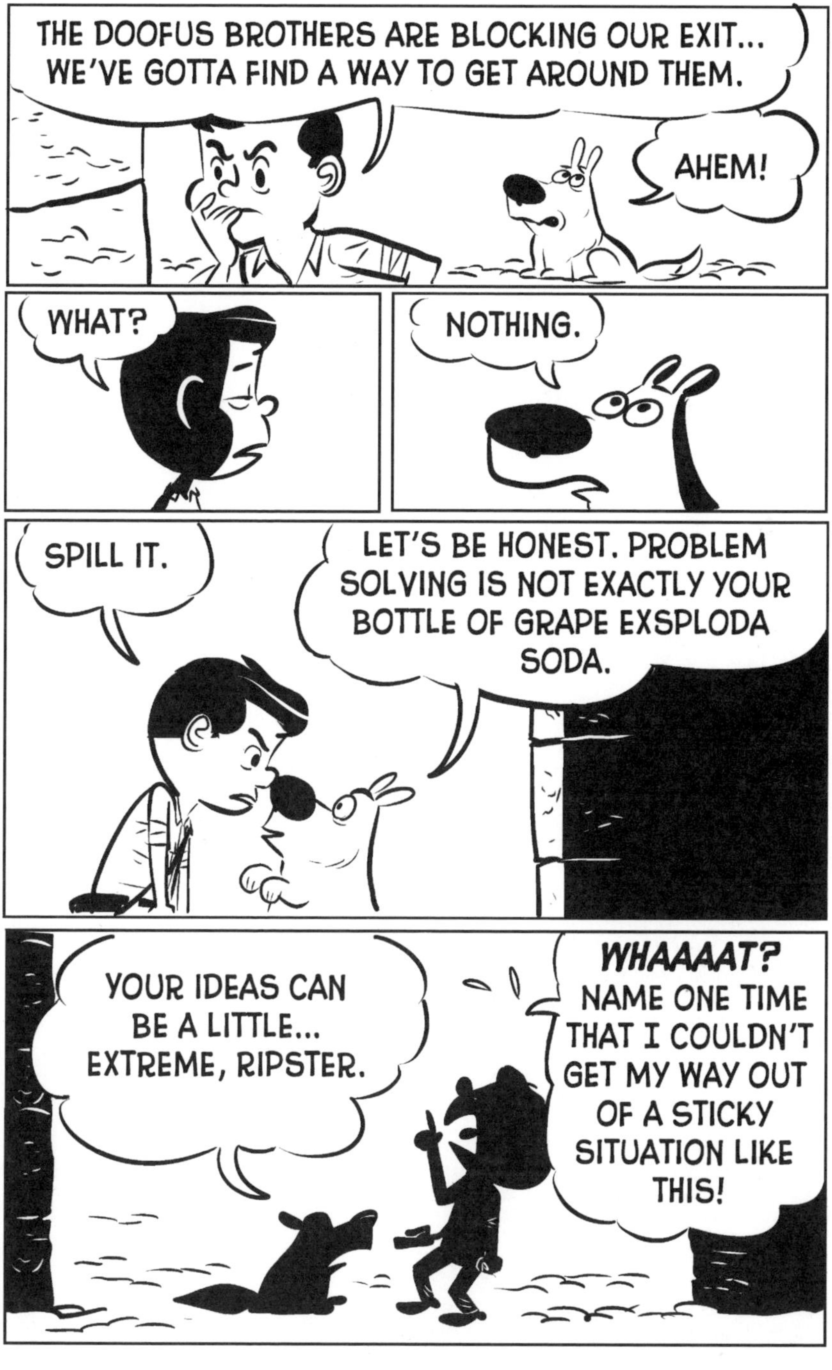
THE DOOFUS BROTHERS ARE BLOCKING OUR EXIT... WE'VE GOTTA FIND A WAY TO GET AROUND THEM.
AHEM!
WHAT?
NOTHING.
SPILL IT.
LET'S BE HONEST. PROBLEM SOLVING IS NOT EXACTLY YOUR BOTTLE OF GRAPE EXSPLODA SODA.
YOUR IDEAS CAN BE A LITTLE... EXTREME, RIPSTER.
WHAAAAT? NAME ONE TIME THAT I COULDN'T GET MY WAY OUT OF A STICKY SITUATION LIKE THIS!

"Let me see, there was . . . that time you thought it would be a good idea to take a shortcut through the lava of a Hawaiian volcano."

IT DIDN'T LOOK ANY HOTTER THAN MY DAD'S CHILI.

"Or that time you thought it was a good idea to escape through the cave of grizzly bears in the Yukon."

I COULD'VE SWORN THEY HIBERNATED IN THE SUMMER.

"And my personal favorite . . . that time when you wanted to swim from Cuba to the United States."

IN MY DEFENSE, IT LOOKED A LOT CLOSER ON THE MAP.

All right, all right. Here's how we tackled this particular problem.

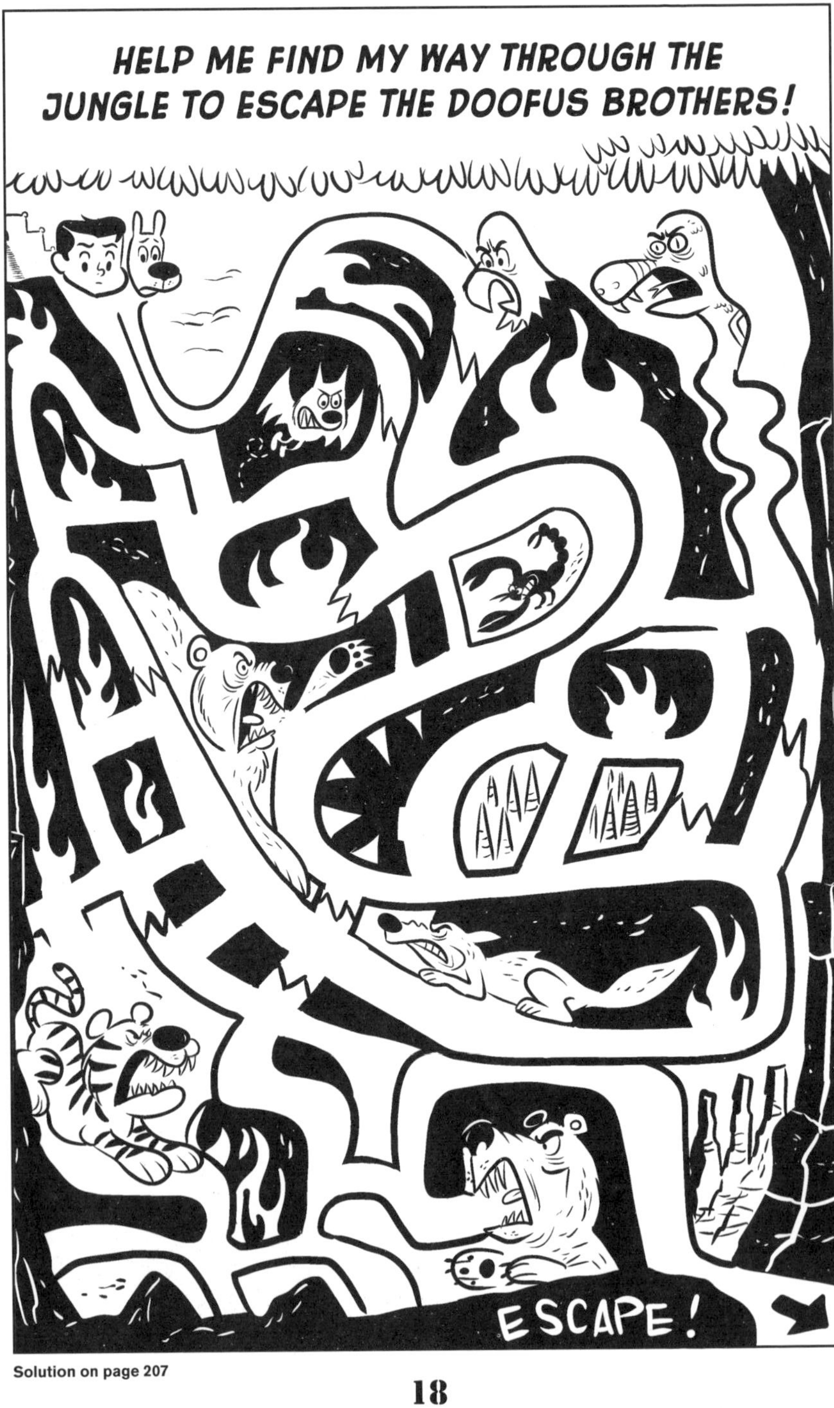
HELP ME FIND MY WAY THROUGH THE JUNGLE TO ESCAPE THE DOOFUS BROTHERS!
ESCAPE!

Solution on page 207

We'd just about escaped, when I saw a cat trapped on a branch hanging over a waterfall! I just had to save the little guy.

The Doofus Brothers were breathing down my neck like Dad when I take too long to throw a grenade after pulling the pin. I had no choice!

I took a photo of the little guy for my Imperiled Animals Scrapbook and headed out on the limb.

I'd just grabbed the soaking wet tabby cat when the Doofus Brothers cut off my escape route. Roofus Doofus yelled, "Hand over the gem, runt!" At least I think it was Roofus. I have to admit, I'm not really sure which one of them is which. TNT begged me to give them the gem. I didn't have much choice. Even the kitty meowed something that sounded like "Give them the gem, mister!" I reached into my backpack to hand over the treasure when the tree branch we were on snapped!

19

We dropped into the mighty waterfall pretty fast. I barely got out a "Wheee!" before we hit the river and water was burning its way up my nose.

TNT was the first one up and out of the water. I would have totally beat him to shore if I hadn't been searching for the little kitty, who'd slipped out of my grasp when we hit the pool below the falls. I couldn't see much underwater, and was about to give up hope when I felt something sharp dig into my shoulder.

It felt like a gigantic mutant freshwater squid with radio-active fangs the size of baseball bats and fire-shooting tentacles.

I got ready to fight to the death, but it turned out to just be a small, soggy cat with really sharp claws. Of all the rotten luck.

So we finally get back with the stupid gem, smelling like wet dingoes in the Outback and scratched all to heck—thanks, Kitty—And what happens?

My dad nabs the gem from my grip and then walks over to this snooty little girl who looks like the genie from *Aladdin* or something. Dad then hands her the gem! Dad told me the gem was a gift for this little girl's birthday, who is . . . I guess . . . the princess of Tango Boom Bango.

She must have gotten a lot of gems for her birthday, because as soon as she saw me, she said:

POST JOURNAL NOTE
By the way, I did a background check and I guess she can keep her crown.

MY KITTY! YOU FOUND MY KITTY!

P-YOW!

This is why I don't have many friends my own age. It really bothers my dad.

My dad is always trying to get me to do things I don't want to do.

(On a personal note to the ladies: I was just kidding about the first two.)

All right, all right! Maybe spending time with kids my age is something I should do, but I just don't have anything in common with them!

I'm starting to think Dad only gave me this mission so he could get me into that princess's birthday bash!

Speaking of gems, these were the highlights of my fun time at the party:

I LIKE RUNNING FROM JUNGLE SAVAGES WHO SPIT POISON DARTS AT ME WHILE I ESCAPE WITH LOST TREASURE.

I LIKE EATING SOUR GUMMI WORMS AND SOMETIMES REAL WORMS.

ONE TIME I SWAM TO A SUBMARINE TO RESCUE...

KA-BURP!

GRAPE EXSPLODA SODA IS MY FAVORITE. I CAN SQUIRT IT THROUGH MY FRONT TEETH.

WHAT IN THE...

WATCH ME PICK MY NOSE AND EAT IT.

I watched him eat his booger. It was a good example of how the rest of the party was going for me.

Later, when the kid making the arm fart sounds finished, I applauded and then snuck away to a quiet place to scarf down a giant slice of cake. Cake is the one reason I will stick it out at a lame birthday party.

It was then that my dad found me, gave me that disappointed look, and asked, "Geez, Rip, why are you sitting here all alone?"

I, being skilled in multiple languages, my favorite being "burplish," chugged some Grape Exsploda Soda and belched out my answer.

It sounded way cooler with the grape aftertaste.

It was then that Dad dropped a bomb on me, and not the fun kind that makes noise and destroys stuff. (Though it did destroy my day.)

BU (I DUNNO) URP!

NO, DAD! DON'T SAY IT! PLEEEASE! NOOOOOO!

OOOOO!

RIP, NOW THAT SUMMER IS HERE, I'VE DECIDED YOU NEED TO HANG OUT WITH NORMAL KIDS. I'M SENDING YOU TO SUMMER CAMP.

SUMMER CAMP!?

No! That's like a 24/7 birthday party, but without the cake!

"Listen, kid, if you don't make the best of it and have some friendly learning experiences with your camp chums, I'll have no choice but to put you in a real school in the fall," the monster who'd replaced my father said.

I then gave my response.

AUUGHHH!

CHAPTER 2

HACK!

After my tonsils called it quits from the screaming, I accepted my doom—spending a few weeks in summer camp. How bad could it be? I've been through worse.

GHOSTS FROM AN OLD MINING TOWN CHASING ME FOR TAKING THEIR HIDDEN GOLD NUGGETS!

IT'S NOT MY FAULT IF THEY "PAN" HANLDE IT!

FIGHTING GREAT WHITE SHARKS INSIDE A SUNKEN PIRATE SHIP!

ARRRR YOU SERIOUS?

Dad made a few calls, and after a few weeks of dread and a couple humdrum missions—thwarting a cyborg supervillain and finding a lost city of gold—the awful day of departure arrived. After a long drive, during which Dad blindfolded me to keep me from knowing where the camp was, we came to a stop. Dad undid the blindfold, shoved me out of the car, and took off like a mutant squid was chasing him. My heart sinking, I followed the signs to the camp office, which turned out to be a small yellow building with pink explosions painted all over it.

I thought this was weird but tried to keep an open mind. Maybe the explosions were pink due to a high concentration of potassium in the bombs.

It happens.

I entered the office and reported to a lady behind a desk. She was sipping a cup of tea and humming "Someday My Prince Will Come."

As I looked around the room, I saw more of the pink explosions, but smaller and with glittery hearts and butterflies around them. That's when it hit me . . . Those weren't explosions. They were flowers! At this point, I began to worry. What if this was a camp for lunatics?

The lady looked at me like I was from outer space and then said the battiest thing ever.

Instead of answering my question, she introduced herself as Florence Finkman, and then picked up a phone. She dialed a number, and, after a short pause, she declared:

I wondered what this was all about and what made me so exciting. Could my reputation already be making me a legend?

I was sure that was it, because what else could it be? I bet that they'll want me to teach classes in kung fu.

I looked out through the flowery curtains to see three ladies zipping by. You could hear the wooden deck creak as they leaped like gazelles running from a pack of wolves.

They all came in and stood near the door, looking at me and giggling. It must have been contagious, because Florence Finkman started to chuckle, too. This must have been the first time they were ever in the presence of an adventurer like myself. I wondered if Indiana Jones went through this. It was then that I was let in on the joke.

I tried desperately to wrap my head around the words that had just punched me in the face harder than a swinging log booby trap!

This had to be some kind of mistake! My dad would never do this to me. Or would he? The stinker!

Florence Finkman must not have ever heard a little boy scream so loud at the thought of spending the summer exclusively with a flock of girls.

No wonder Dad had left me on my own so suddenly. He knew what kind of disaster he was leading me into.

See if I ever save him from a pack of feral tigers again.

Florence Finkman and the others tried to cheer me up by changing the subject.

They told me that one of the campers had a birthday today. If I could guess her age, I'd get a donut from the counselors' lunchroom.

GUESS HER AGE

You can guess this camper's age from the clues in this number puzzle.

CLUES
It is a number between 1 and 10.
It is an odd number.
It is more than 3.
It is not 7 minus 2.
It is not 4 plus 5.

Solution on page 207

As I tried to work out the math, I was reminded of the time I snuck aboard a pirate ship sailing in Blood Diamond Bay.

Dad and I were on an adventure to retrieve a rare diamond that was stolen by none other than Black Nose the Pirate. Do you like that name? I'm the one who gave it to that stupid buccaneer.

Black Nose's real name was Dave, but Dave the Pirate doesn't really strike fear on the seven seas.

I was still years away from ninjalike stealth, and the pirates heard me coming a mile away. I was also really hungry, and probably shouldn't have started eating my big bag of Chile Limón Funyuns: But salty snacks are a must before any serious fight. Nutrition!

Black Nose's goons were closing in. All of a sudden, the dreaded pirate himself cornered me, brandishing a ham sandwich!

I guess he was eating when his goons sounded the alarm, and he picked up his sandwich instead of his sword. When I noticed the sandwich was only ham and mustard, I said in my smoothest James Bond–like voice …

I took a flying leap and went over his head, pushing him to the ground. He landed square on an open bottle of ink!

Then I threw a knife, cutting in half a rope that was holding a giant safe twenty feet off the ground, which came crashing down and sank the pirate ship.

The safe smashed through the ship's hull and sank into the bay. My dad found it using his awesome mini-submarine, and inside the safe was . . . wait for it . . . the diamond!

After I told that very true story to myself, I was still stuck trying to figure out the camper's age. And what was worse was those donuts smelled really good.

It was then I glanced back at her and noticed she had an open birthday card in her backpack, and I could make out the number . . .

The ladies looked at me in awe. Except for Miss Finkman, who mostly looked sad because she was hoping to have one more maple Long John.

I was then sent up PowderPuff Trail to my cottage on Unicorn Boulevard.

I guess the moral of this story and the run-in with Pirate Black Nose was that sometimes when the odds are against you, you just get lucky.

CHAPTER 3

I won't lie: As I unpacked my stuff, I felt pretty down. I could almost hear the cooties gnawing their way through my cabin walls. But then I thought that if I could handle the lost tribe of the Toe-Eating People, I could handle a bunch of girls.

Since I would need all my strength, I immediately took a long nap. Plenty of sleep is a soldier of fortune necessity. I slept into the evening, and woke up to the smell of a campfire and the sound of kids singing over the hill.

I decided to make a big entrance by running over and backflipping in. When in doubt, backflip: that's what I always say.

While I limbered up my muscles for sweet acrobatic stunts, I thought of the time Dad and I visited the desert city of Ari-Boo-Boo.

I'd had to sneak into the palace of Sneakum Abu, a ruthless, evil wizard who had cast a spell on the entire town. He magically forced every citizen to chew his brand of Sneakum bubble gum. This madman had to be stopped. (It was really horrible gum.)

Dad told me the spell could be broken by locating and destroying the powerful medallion that the wizard Sneakum had used to cast it.

He told me that he had learned the medallion was hidden in a snake pit filled with nine deadly king cobras, but that one king cobra was actually a fake and I would need to spot the difference. If I could do that, I would find the medallion hidden inside the fake cobra.

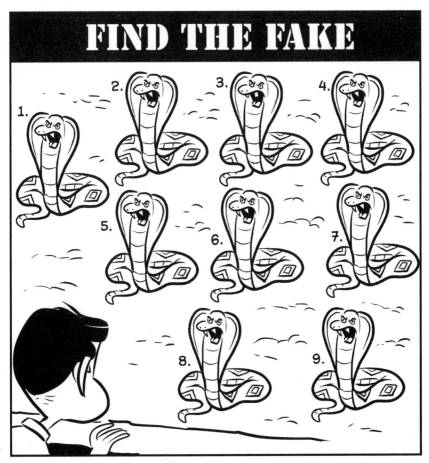

Solution on page 207

Once I figured out which snake was fake, I grabbed my handy snake-charming flute and hypnotized the reptiles with a little tune.

I managed to grab the medallion, but my flute playing set off an alarm, and Sneakum's henchmen came chasing after me on magic flying carpets!

I grabbed a flying carpet that had been parked nearby and zoomed off into the night with the guards in hot pursuit.

I zigzagged all through Ari-Boo-Boo's skyline, trying to lose the bad guys. Luckily, I was the only one who remembered the three rules of flying a magic carpet:

1. Always wear your seat belt!

2. Always look both ways before crossing the clouds!

3. Always make sure that your flying carpet has plenty of fuel!

Finally, with all the wizard's goons out of the way, it was time to face off with the big man himself! Getting rid of this guy wasn't going to be easy. He made Saruman look like Mickey Mouse!

It was time to bring out the big guns.

When that didn't work, suddenly I was out of rocks and ideas!

The wizard Sneakum chased me until I crashed in the village bazaar. People chewing Sneakum bubble gum surrounded me. Sneakum appeared in front of me.

This was it! I was toast . . . or was I?!

I pulled the medallion out of my pocket and said:

I then smashed the medallion on the ground and it shattered into a million pieces!

The wizard drew his sword to finish me off!

POST JOURNAL NOTE
"Drew" means pulled it out... he didn't actually draw it on a piece of paper.

In the nick of time, the effects of the magic spell wore off . . .

EW!

THIS TASTES LIKE A CAMEL'S SWEAT SOCK!

And the people of Ari-Boo-Boo spit their pieces of gum at the wizard Sneakum. The wads stuck to him, freezing him in place.

The gum hardened lickety-split, and turned the wizard into a statue, which to this day still stands in the center of Ari-Boo-Boo as a warning to all wizards trying to trick the good people.

True story!

So, there I was, getting ready to make a big first impression on my fellow campers.

I started running down the hill, gaining the necessary speed for my backflip extravaganza. Suddenly, I tripped on a rock!

I plummeted down the hill like a boulder down a volcano, and landed KA-PLOP in a mud puddle. I was pretty dizzy from the fall, and couldn't see through all the mud on my face.

That's when I stumbled into a beehive!

Luckily, my armor of stinky mud deflected most of the stings, but a few got through. I'm battle-hardened, though, and kept my cool.

As I ran screaming toward the campfire, I noticed the girls were talking to each other.

This just wasn't my night!

I finally reached the pond and dove in to save myself.

When I got out, I figured someone would at least offer me a towel. Or a s'more. Running from bees makes a guy hungry! But no. All I got was a heaping plate of trouble! Miss Finkman sent me to my cottage and I wasn't allowed to hang out with the campers for the rest of the night. I wasn't even allowed to explain what happened.

It was a total accident. I was the victim!

GUILTY!

They figured I was trying to scare the girls and didn't understand I was actually being beat up by Mother Nature!

I couldn't believe it. Nobody listened to me! It was at that moment that I decided I'd had enough. I made up my mind to escape from Pink PowderPuff Summer Camp!

CHAPTER 4

I had decided to escape from Pink PowderPuff Summer Camp! There was no stopping me.

Luckily, I could always count on my trusty dog for help.

I had learned the hard way the importance of always having an emergency exit.

Dad had once been hired by an archaeologist to protect an old tomb in the desert of Eclipso. Archaeologists are the people who find remnants of lost civilizations and put them in museums. It's sort of like my job but without the booby traps.

Dad was betting that the Doofus Brothers would try to rob the tomb while he was away at a soldier of fortune conference. He left me on guard duty.

Thieves always seem to know when things are unlocked . . . it's almost like they can smell opportunity. Someday, I'll get to go to a soldier of fortune conference instead of doing the grunt work. I bet it'll be at a convention center and everything.

It was getting late and I started to get really tired. That's when I heard footsteps . . . Doofus footsteps.

It was the Doofuses, all right. Sometimes, ancient kings were buried with gold, jewels, and treasure. In my experience, tomb treasure is usually cursed, but that doesn't stop Doofuses.

I tried to call for backup, but the tomb walls were interfering with my walkie-talkie's reception. I wish Dad would get me a cell phone.

Through really, really dumb luck, the Doofuses had stumbled on a secret chamber.

Inside the chamber was a golden coffin, along with a whole bunch of old loot.

On the wall of the chamber, there were some ominous hieroglyphs. Hieroglyphic writing was an ancient system that came in especially handy for writing curses.

Many of the hieroglyphs were simple pictures of the things they referred to, but they could also be symbols for sounds.

The Doofus Brothers could barely get through a Dr. Seuss book, so these hieroglyphs were blowing their minds.

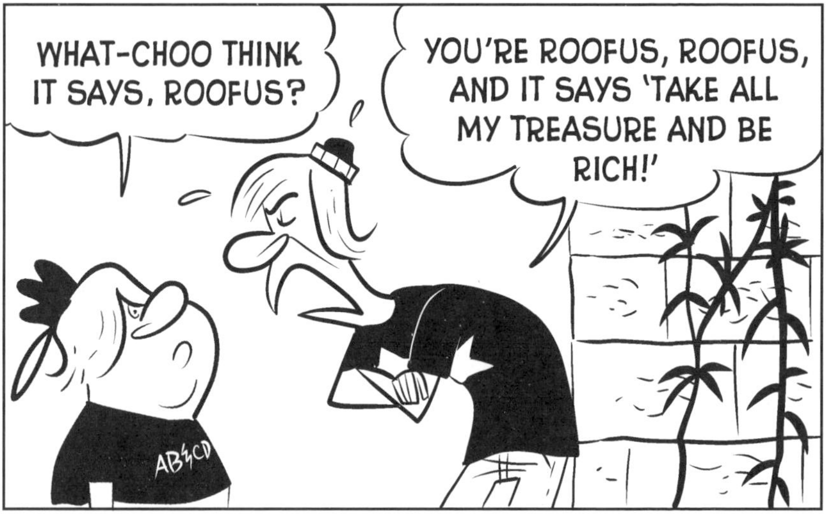
WHAT-CHOO THINK IT SAYS, ROOFUS?
YOU'RE ROOFUS, ROOFUS, AND IT SAYS 'TAKE ALL MY TREASURE AND BE RICH!'

I could smell a curse coming, but it was too late to escape. Suddenly, the walls started to shake and the ceiling collapsed with a roar. It went dark, and everything was quiet. Until:

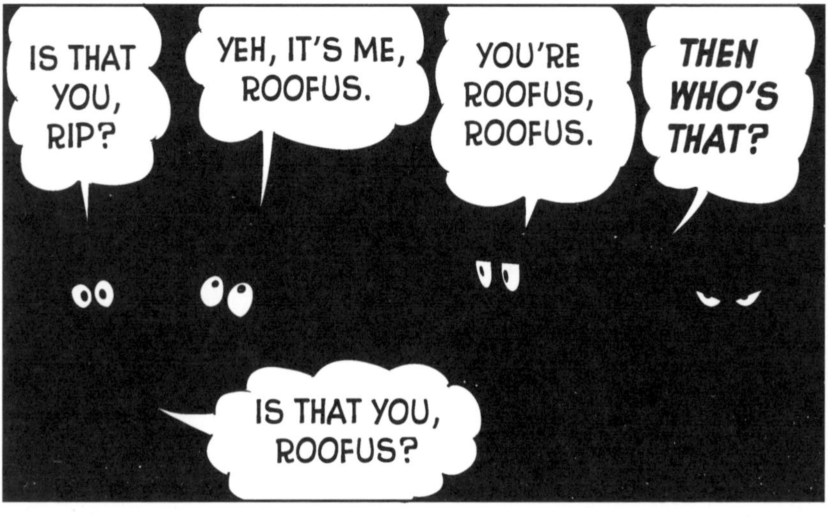
IS THAT YOU, RIP?
YEH, IT'S ME, ROOFUS.
YOU'RE ROOFUS, ROOFUS.
THEN WHO'S THAT?
IS THAT YOU, ROOFUS?

I reached into my backpack and found my flashlight.

I shut my flashlight off!

For a terrible minute or two, I thought I was going to die with the two biggest morons in the known universe.

The tomb's collapse had sealed off the exit! It looked like we were doomed. Luckily, cursed mummies walk really slowly. Much like me before I've had my breakfast in the morning.

As I ran around a dark corner, I noticed a gleam of light on the floor. It was from the moon! This could lead to our way out.

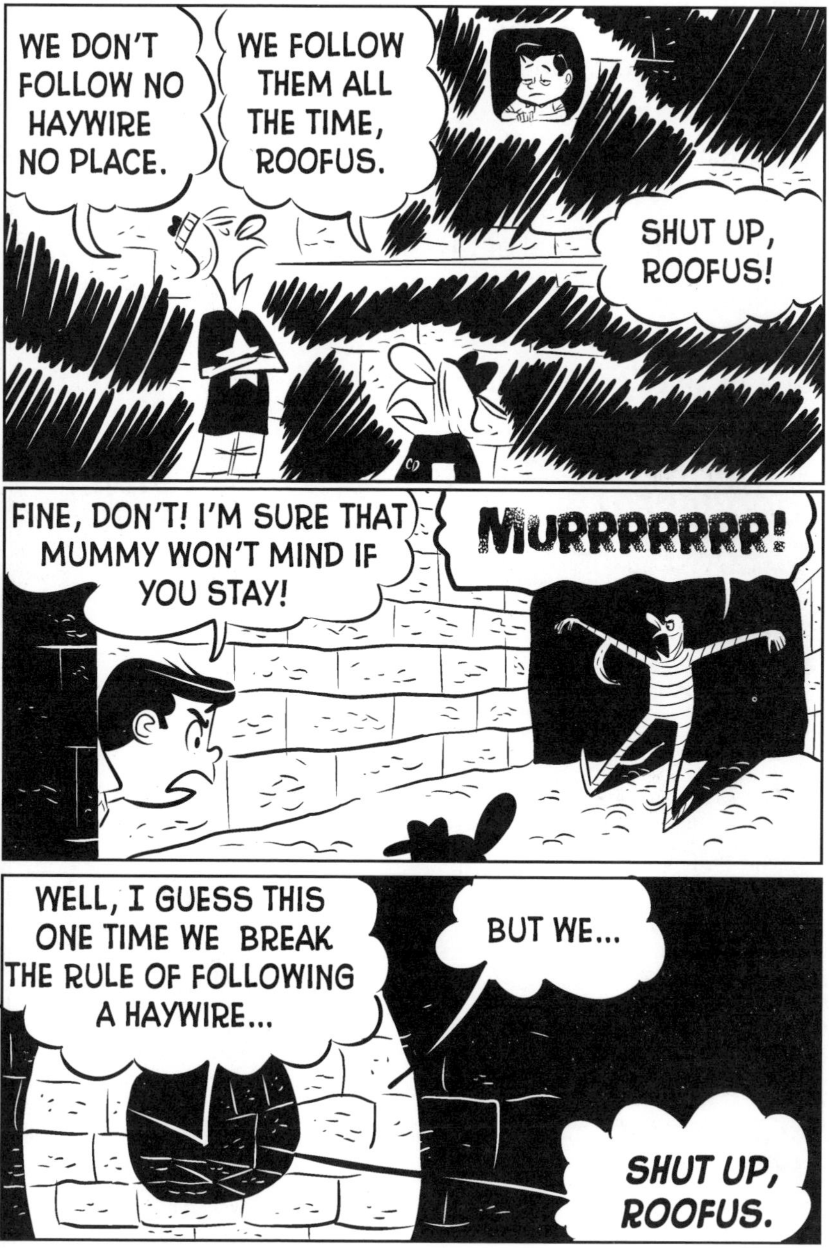
WE DON'T FOLLOW NO HAYWIRE NO PLACE.
WE FOLLOW THEM ALL THE TIME, ROOFUS.
SHUT UP, ROOFUS!
FINE, DON'T! I'M SURE THAT MUMMY WON'T MIND IF YOU STAY!
MURRRRRRR!
WELL, I GUESS THIS ONE TIME WE BREAK THE RULE OF FOLLOWING A HAYWIRE...
BUT WE...
SHUT UP, ROOFUS.

We followed the gleam of light down a dank tunnel, the mummy in slow pursuit. We came to a fork in the road. I went one way and the Doofuses disappeared down the other path. Good riddance. They could do the mummy's laundry for eternity, as far as I was concerned. Finally, I came to a small hole in the wall of the tomb that I managed to squeeze through. As soon as I was free, the tomb crumbled completely, sinking back into the desert, along with all its treasure and curses. Typically, Dad blamed me for the tomb's destruction.

At Camp Pinka-Stink (my new nickname for the place),
I at least didn't have a mummy following me. I took a look
around. The place was more like a prison than a camp. There
was no way out.

It had walls ten feet tall with barbed wire on the top!

Guard towers with searchlights!

Vicious dog patrols!

If it weren't for all the psycho girls, Camp Pink Powder-Puff would be a pretty safe place. But getting out was going to be a challenge.

I didn't realize how tough it was going to be until I tripped over what I thought was a squirrel. It turned out to be a decoy that tripped an alarm.

As the alarm sounded, I made a mad dash back to my cottage and leaped under the covers of my bed.

Before I went to bed, I wrote a list of three possible ways to escape and what might go wrong with each of them.

1. Hot air balloon.

Pros: Allows you to laugh aloud at your victorious escape as you soar away into the big blue sky. A good opportunity to spit on the heads of your foes.

Cons: Easily shot down by flying squirrels launched out of cannons.

KA-SQUIRREL!

KA-BOOM!

2. Digging under fence.

Pros: Simple and involves lots of dirt.

Cons: Vulnerable to attack by laser-shooting groundhog soldiers!

3. Hijack a camp truck and jump over the fence!

Pros: No cooler way to escape.

Cons: Truck likely a Transformer that would put me in time-out.

I was sunk. If I didn't figure out a way to escape, I'd be stuck here for the summer doing all types of things that would make my skin crawl!

1. Horseback riding.

2. Canoeing.

I could not allow these awful things to happen to me. I had to get out! But how? I was going to have to dig deep into my soldier of fortune playbook and do something I'd never done before, something so crazy and drastic, I wasn't sure that I could do it and not lose my mind. I'd have to pretend to be a normal kid.

CHAPTER 5

Escape was not going to be easy. If I wanted out of here, I was going to need help. And that meant talking to other campers. Luckily, my spy training taught me how to smoothly infiltrate an enemy base.

I asked around a few more times and realized this was going to be tougher than I thought. Turns out that even hardened thugs have nothing on tween girls! One thing was for sure: I was going to need some breakfast. I headed over to the mess hall for some chow.

The dining room was full of girls talking and laughing. Until they saw me. Then it went dead quiet.

The silence worried me . . . I like crunchy cereal, and I make a lot of noise when I chew. I was looking for the Sugar Punches when a girl the size of a tank stopped me. According to some hushed whispers I heard behind me, this ribboned colossus was Big Bernice. I'm not sure why kids called her that . . . she wasn't any bigger than the werewolf zombie I beat at Pokémon last winter.

I kept my cool. OK, I was sweating, but even ice melts in these summer temperatures. I glared back at her and waited for this monster-sized elephant girl to speak.

Finally, someone was speaking my language! A good fight was just the sort of thing I needed to relax. Once the campers saw me stand up to this gargantuan bully, I'd be the most popular kid around.

Big Bernice quietly grew a few feet, and the giant hams on the ends of her arms clenched ominously. But that wasn't what worried me.

The roomful of girls, instead of waiting in suppressed awe for me to teach Big Bernice a lesson, quietly gathered behind her, staring daggers my way. That's when it hit me: They were all on Bernice's side! She wasn't the bully—I was! The whole world stopped.

Even the crickets out in the grass shut up.

This was my choice: I could either lay some serious junior soldier of fortune hurt on girl-gorilla here and get torn apart by a mob of angry ladies, or take a Buick-sized fist to my pretty face!

I had to think of something . . .

I flashed back to when Dad and I were searching for pirate treasure in the Caribbean.

We'd found the sunken ship of Dyed Beard the Pirate. Supposedly, his boat had had a ton of booty on board when it hit a submerged reef. Dyed Beard was probably texting and sailing.

Finding the ship wasn't hard, but I felt like I was being watched.

The ship had a secure vault with some kind of puzzle lock that wouldn't open unless you solved it. I wish I had this kind of lock for my bike!

BREAK THE CODE!

QJSBUFT   TNFMM   XPSTF
PIRATES SMELL   WORSE

UIBO   TUJOLZ   TLVOLT!
THAN STINKY SKUNKS!

FOUFS   BU   ZPVS   PXO   SJTL!
_ _ _ _   _ _   _ _ _ _   _ _ _   _ _ _ _ !

Solution on page 207

The vault opened, and inside was enough treasure to make Scrooge McDuck blush. I started to head up to tell Dad when I saw a great white shark clearly in the mood for a Rip-sized value meal!

This shark was being a real bully. Just because he had three rows of razor-sharp teeth didn't mean he could pick on this kid!

That's right, you don't need glasses or better glasses—I punched that shark right in his pointy snoot!

The great white had never expected me to fight back.

I then proceeded to bite him to see how he liked it!

I sent that shark packing, all right. He was waiting for the bus back to his mommy when I swam away.

But I couldn't do that to Big Bernice. Biting her would only give the angry mob of girls some ideas.

I was in serious trouble. Maybe it was time for the nuclear option, something I'd never done before, or thought I would do. Apologize.

I started to say, "I'm sorry, girls," but my mouth refused to cooperate.

TAKE A STEP CLOSER, AND YOU'RE GOING TO BE DRINKING YOUR UGLY JUICE THROUGH A STRAW FOR A WEEK!

I was just about to get clobbered when Miss Finkman walked into the mess hall. I never thought I'd be glad to see her!

I could tell that she'd sized up the situation and knew what needed to be done: lock up Big Bernice for trying to tear off my innocent head.

I was still working on that apology.
I met my fate with the quiet dignity of a trained warrior!

As my jailer dragged me out of the mess hall, something weird happened.

This little redheaded girl bumped into me and slipped something into my pocket.

Miss Finkman took me to her office and gave me a bran muffin to eat. I could see the torture was already beginning. Miss Finkman watched me as I struggled to swallow my horrifying breakfast. I could tell she was planning her line of attack. I would have to be careful. If her opening move was a bran muffin, she meant business.

How could I tell her that these girls were animals? They were out for blood! I was just trying to survive. I bit into my muffin as slowly as I could. I could tell it was starting to get to Miss Finkman.

She yelled out, **"ARE YOU DONE YET?"**
I responded:

I finally somehow finished my muffin and calmly waited for Finkman to begin her torture. She started by listing all the trouble I had caused since I got there. I must admit, I wasn't expecting her to use guilt. She was a better enemy than I thought.

MR. HAYWIRE, YOU'VE BEEN A TERROR TO ALL THE CAMPERS!

LITTLE SUZIE BECKMAN IS NOW AFRAID TO LEAVE HER TENT BECAUSE OF THE MUD MONSTER!

SUZIE, PLEASE COME OUT FROM UNDER THE BED.

NEVER! YOU COULD BE ONE OF THEM!

AND USING BEES IN YOUR SCHEMES! THEY SHOULD BE MAKING DELICIOUS HONEY, NOT STINGING LIZZIE AND GRETCHEN! AND HONESTLY, EVEN I DON'T ANTAGONIZE BIG BERNICE!

WHY DO YOU HATE IT HERE, SON? IF YOU GIVE US A CHANCE, WE COULD HAVE SO MUCH FUN! COMING UP, WE'VE GOT ...

CAMPFIRE SONGS...

ARTS AND CRAFTS...

HIKING...

HORSEBACK RIDING.

Her technique was unexpectedly good, but it was going to take more than guilt to break Rip Haywire!

CHAPTER 6

I was feeling pretty down about things when I remembered the map that the redheaded girl had given me. Maybe there was one person in the camp who didn't think I was the worst. I pulled out the map, which turned out to actually be a puzzle.

It was some kind of secret way to find her. Maybe you could help me out with this one?

Solution on page 207

She must be down by the animal petting zoo. Why a camp would have all this stuff and not one single bazooka range is beyond me.

I walked into the petting area, and there she was.

She looked pretty cool . . . for a girl.

She had nice red hair. It reminded me of explosions.

My soldier of fortune judgment led me to believe that here was someone who could keep her cool when things went south. And then she tripped on a rock and totally lost it.

OK, maybe I was wrong about keeping her cool.

AHHH! I JUST GOT MANURE ON MY FAVORITE SHOES!

Lucky for this girl's shoes, it wasn't manure, just some crushed-up chow pellets. After she calmed down, we got down to business.

I played it cool until I got more information. If Dad could see me now, he'd be all like . . .

It all had to do with her granddad. He was an explorer who specialized in finding lost treasure, so he sounded like my kind of guy.

Once, while looking in a bookstore for some old *Plastic Man* comics, he found an ancient map hidden in the back of an *Amazing Spider-Man*. It showed the way to a treasure hidden in an old Native American pyramid. Breezy said that it was the very same pyramid that we were going to visit in a couple weeks!

Of course, looking for treasure was probably not on the field trip agenda. This camp just gets everything wrong.

Evidently, this girl's granddad had gotten arthritis and was forced to retire before he had a chance to find the treasure.

The thought of this treasure haunted her granddad. He couldn't stand being stuck golfing, bowling, fishing, and winning at bingo when he could be enduring awful hardships and risking his life to find a big honking pile of dusty gold.

I almost caved. She seemed so excited at the prospect of danger. I liked that about her, but I liked my freedom more.

This was pretty tempting. No one except Dad had ever asked for my help before. And Dad never offered me something in exchange, except for a promised machete for Christmas (hopefully). But I couldn't see working with a partner. It would only slow me down.

It was then that I had a change of heart. Breezy had cried out almost all the water in her body; she was in mortal danger of dehydration! I had to say yes and save her life!

She was a sweet kid. She couldn't stop thanking me.

There was about a week until the big field trip to the temple. Since I was assured of escape after that, I decided that I might as well make the most of Pink PowderPuff Summer Camp. Plus, I needed to blend in to deflect suspicion.

I signed up for a load of activities and, well, let's just say they went as well as everything else so far . . .

Arts and crafts:

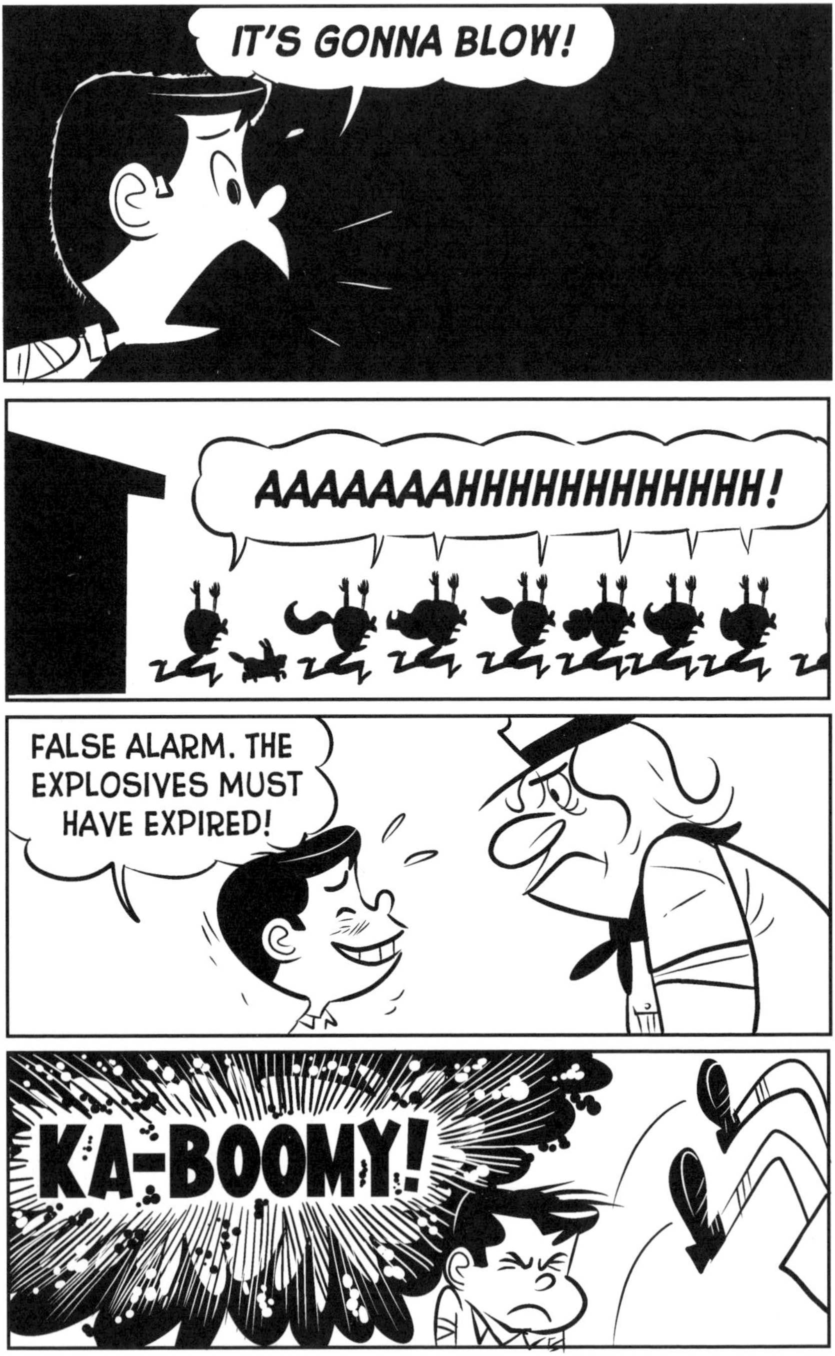
IT'S GONNA BLOW!
AAAAAAAHHHHHHHHHHHHH!
FALSE ALARM. THE EXPLOSIVES MUST HAVE EXPIRED!
KA-BOOMY!

Chorus:

Solo? The only solo I wanted anything to do with was the pilot of the Millennium Falcon in *Star Wars*!

Fishing:

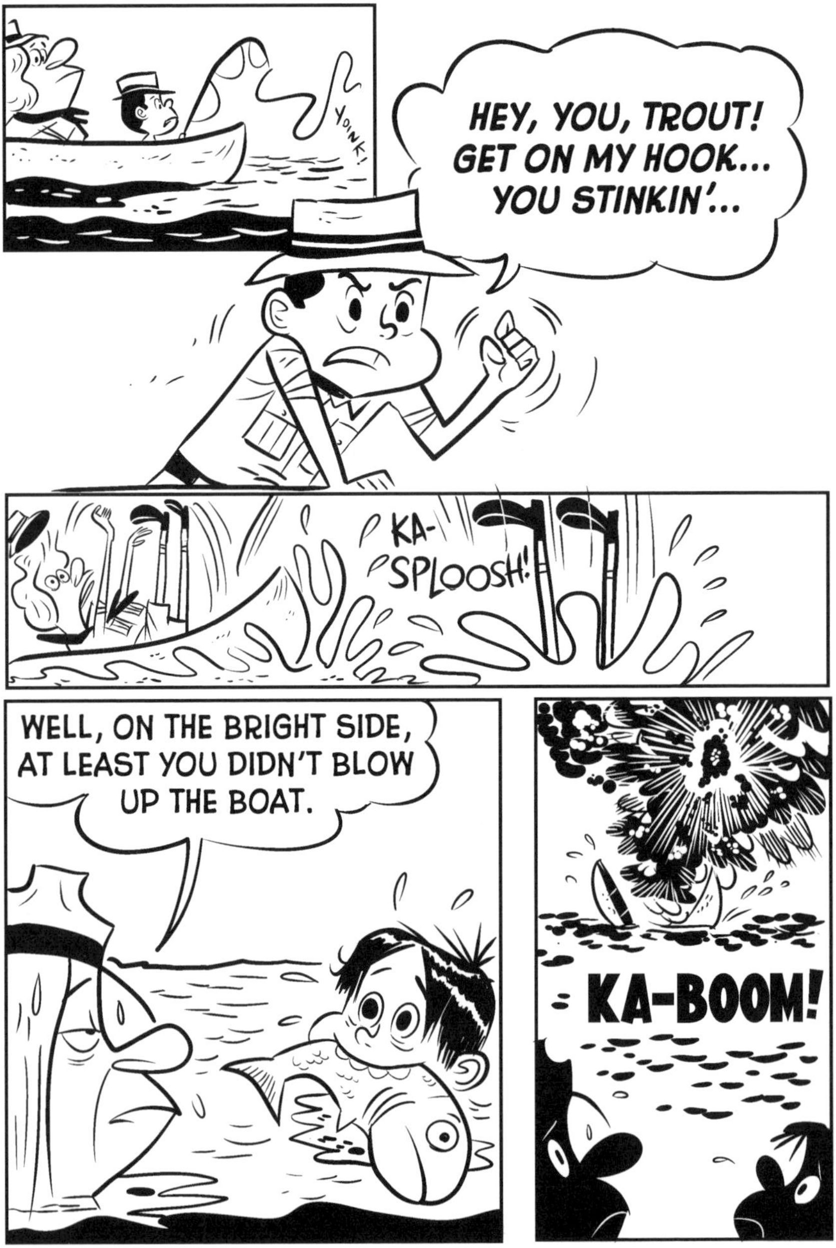
YOINK!
HEY, YOU, TROUT! GET ON MY HOOK... YOU STINKIN'...
KA-SPLOOSH!
WELL, ON THE BRIGHT SIDE, AT LEAST YOU DIDN'T BLOW UP THE BOAT.
KA-BOOM!

Writing letters to my dad:

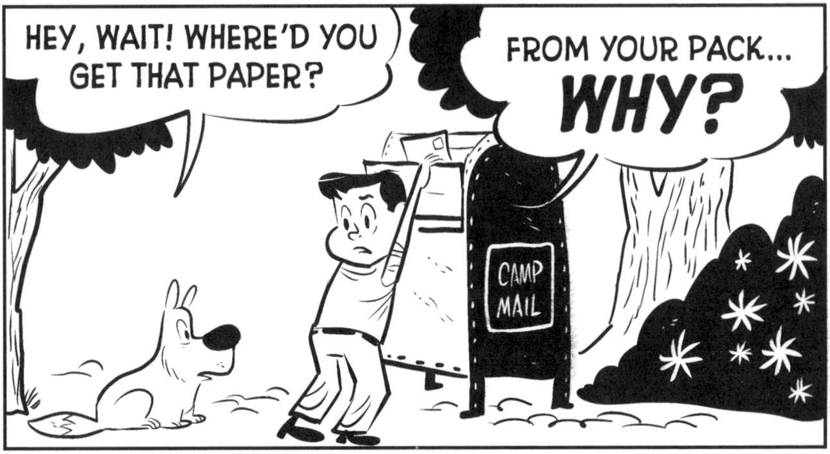
HEY, WAIT! WHERE'D YOU GET THAT PAPER?
FROM YOUR PACK... WHY?
CAMP MAIL

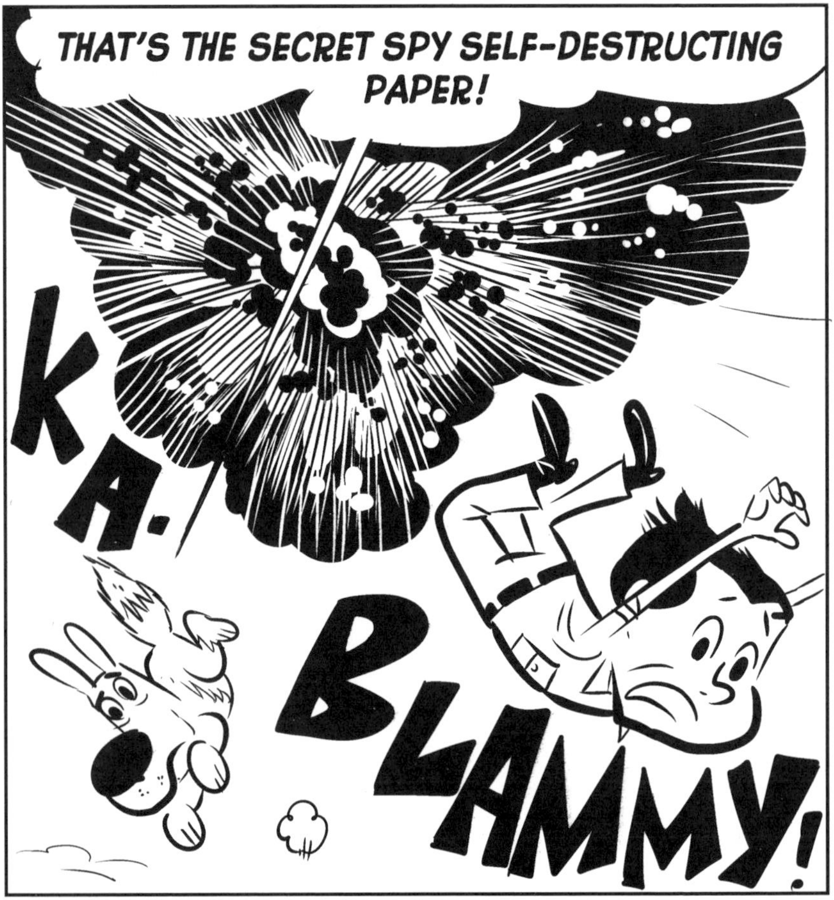
THAT'S THE SECRET SPY SELF-DESTRUCTING PAPER!
KA-BLAMMY!

Now I know why some kids get so sad at summer camp!

They give you a hard time for every little thing!

CHAPTER 7

Yesterday was not one of my best.

I couldn't understand! I've driven a nuclear-powered tank safely off a cliff, but I couldn't handle a camp full of girls? What was wrong with me?

If I have to be totally honest . . . driving a tank is easier than making friends.

I SURRENDER!

The thing was, I was starting to see what made kids think summer camp was so much fun. It gave me a chance to sharpen my painting, fishing, and horseback riding skills without the pressure of fearing for my life. I didn't even mind that there was no bomb-making class! I even thought that I wouldn't mind learning to dance!

Don't laugh! Dad says boxers take dancing lessons to learn balance, rhythm, and timing.

But I wasn't going to work on any of that stuff if I kept making a mess of everything. I couldn't even do the one thing I was sent here to do—make friends. And I've made friends with mole-people who were allergic to humans!

MISSION FAILURE

I needed to take a hard look at what I was doing and try to fix it.

Less about myself? I couldn't even begin to understand TNT's new age mumbo jumbo. What else should I think about? Karate? How could I impress the girls if I wasn't focusing on my awesomeness?

Maybe there was a tiny kernel of truth to my dog's nonsensical ravings. Whatever I was doing, it wasn't working. But is it my fault I always do things the hard way? I just can't say no to a challenge!

How was I going to make friends with these girls if they just wouldn't see all my amazing qualities and death-defying skills?

ALL I WANT TO DO IS SHOW THEM HOW MUCH COOLER I AM THAN THEY ARE! WHY WON'T THEY SEE IT?

OOOH! I'VE BEEN A TOTAL SHOW-OFFY JERK BAG!

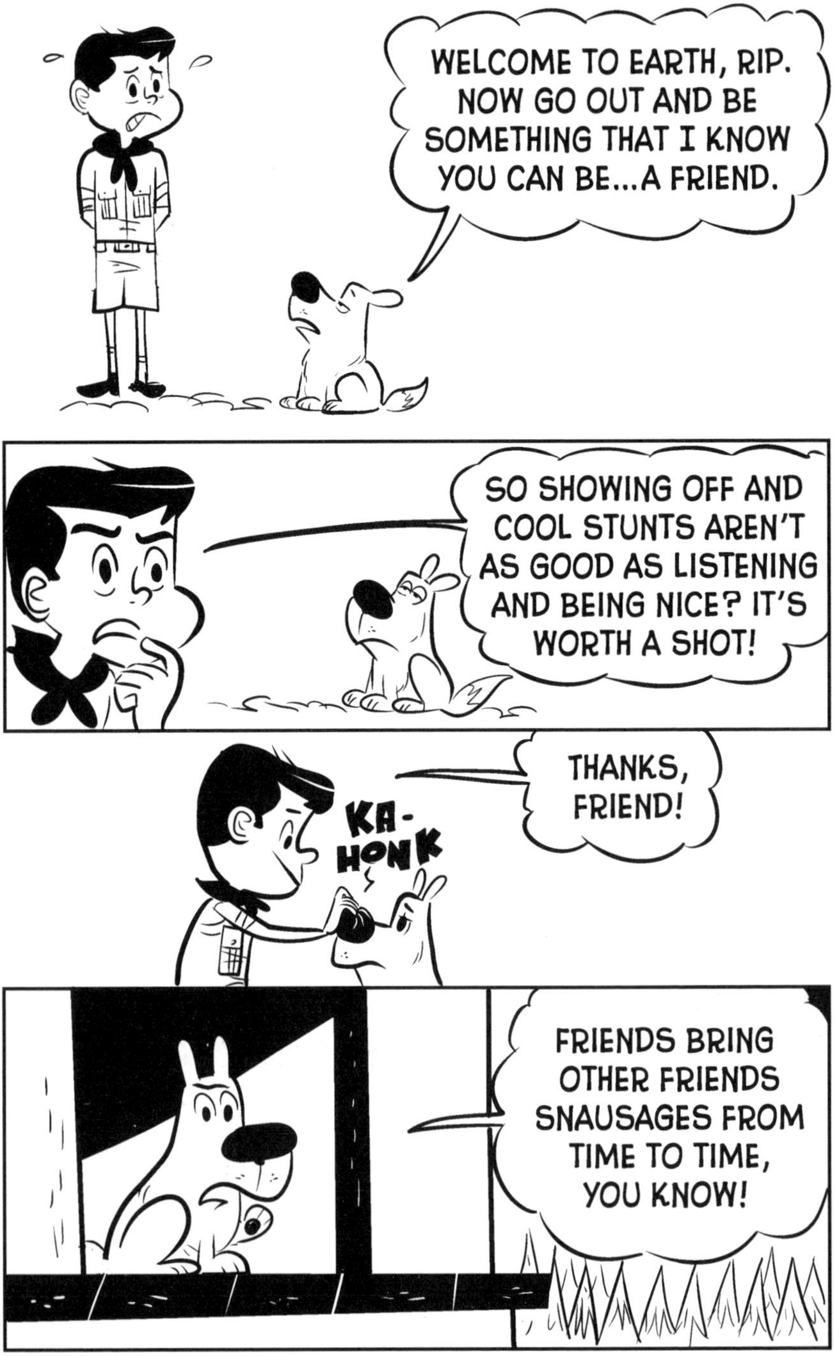
WELCOME TO EARTH, RIP. NOW GO OUT AND BE SOMETHING THAT I KNOW YOU CAN BE...A FRIEND.
SO SHOWING OFF AND COOL STUNTS AREN'T AS GOOD AS LISTENING AND BEING NICE? IT'S WORTH A SHOT!
KA-HONK
THANKS, FRIEND!
FRIENDS BRING OTHER FRIENDS SNAUSAGES FROM TIME TO TIME, YOU KNOW!

I was all set to give this friendship thing a try with the other campers, when suddenly . . .

The next thing I knew, it was five till high noon. I had to face Big Bernice somehow. Now it was time to taste my medicine, and the flavor was revenge.

I had no idea how she would use ice cream as a weapon, but I knew she was going to make it cold and hurty. I just hoped it wasn't low fat.

This challenge reminded me of the time I was in the Highyawayup Mountains on a job rescuing climbers. Dad sent me ahead to scout around. When I finally found the climbers' camp, it was empty! There was nothing there but shredded tents and footprints.

Big ones . . .

It was . . . you guessed it . . . an abominable snowman. I'm not sure what "abominable" means, but it sure doesn't mean super cuddly.

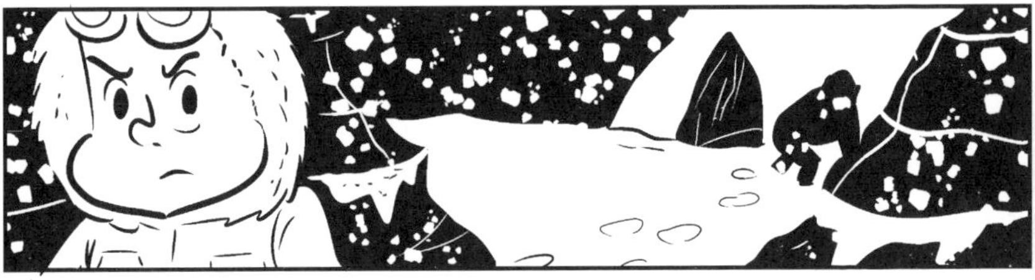

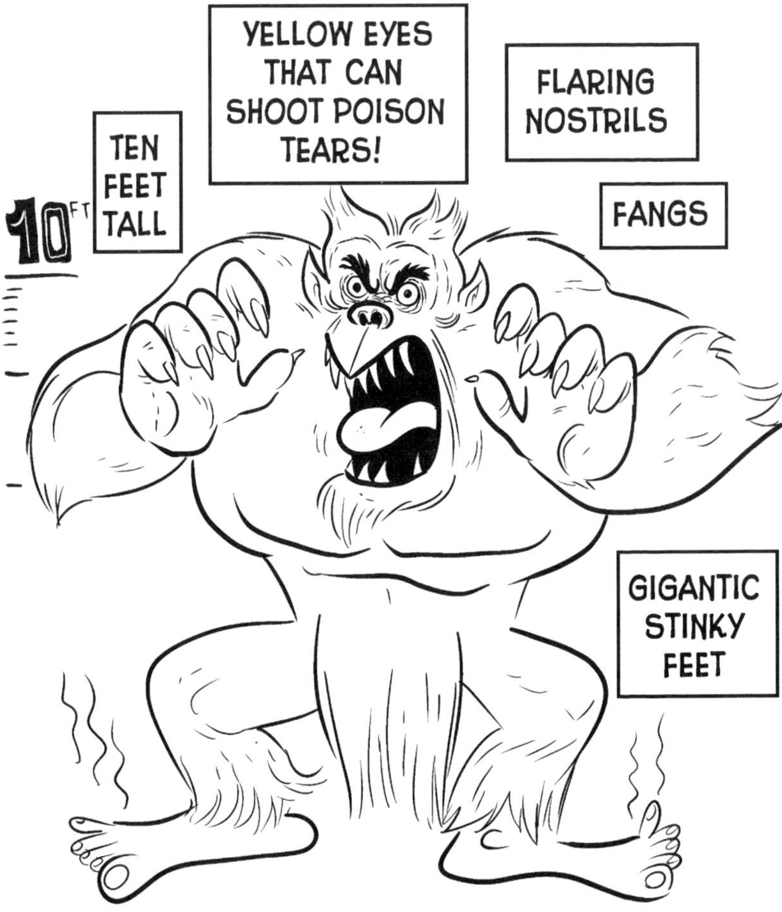
YELLOW EYES THAT CAN SHOOT POISON TEARS!
FLARING NOSTRILS
10FT
TEN FEET TALL
FANGS
GIGANTIC STINKY FEET

I needed to save the mountain climbers, but I had to find their lost supplies and do it without running into the abominable snowman.

Can you help me find a way around him?

MOUNTAIN CLIMBERS

I'm getting ready to rescue the mountain climbers. I'll need a pickax, tent, jackets, and rope. Find a path through the maze to pick up what I need. I can't take more than one of each.

Solution on page 207

Once I helped the climbers escape, I was ready to say, "Mission accomplished!" But just as I opened my mouth, the snowman jumped down behind me. He turned me around and looked me over, probably deciding which part to eat first. He stared at me with an icy glare, but in this weather, everything was icy.

UH– MISSION A-NOT-PLISHED!

They say it's harder to smell things in extreme cold, which means his breath was probably fatal in a normal climate. I was going to have to burn that parka.

Every cell in my body was screaming to run (especially my nose cells—this guy really did stink) but there was no way I could get around this monster.

Just then, my iPad fell out of my pocket and it turned on Minecraft.

It distracted the snowman long enough for me to run  away. Heck, I could have walked away, with plenty of time between steps. As far as I know, he's still up there playing it.

If I was going to get out of this duel with Big Bernice, I knew I'd have to give something up.

In this case, I'd have to give up my pride and let her win, no matter what the cost.

Bernice had challenged me to an ice cream eating contest. Whoever could eat eight scoops the fastest was the winner. I looked around for some chocolate sauce or whipped cream, but didn't see any. Bernice was playing hardball, all right.

Bernice looked like she'd done this before, so it'd be easy to lose to her.

I started off eating pretty slowly, but Bernice was even slower. Maybe her giant jaw made it hard for her to chew.

I choked down one scoop of strawberry, which is my least favorite ice cream flavor. Next up was Choco-Explosion, which is the best. I accidentally gulped it down superfast. How can you not wolf down Choco-Explosion, right?

I was winning! She was barely through her strawberry scoop!

I couldn't believe this! I was going to win! The one time I wanted to lose!

I had no choice . . . I had to do the most dangerous thing you could do when eating ice cream. That's right—I had to give myself a brain freeze!

I shoved four scoops into my mouth at one time.

I could feel my brain turn into a block of ice.

The cold was intense and sudden, but I handled it like a hardened pro.

I began to think I'd gone too far. I'd had more than my head could handle. I was losing my mind!

I raced out of the mess hall, hoping the sun would melt away the pain!

As I lay flat on the ground, brain-flavored slushie juice seeped out of my ears.

I could hear the campers cheer on Big Bernice for her win. Things were starting to look up!

Well, to be fair, everything looks better after a really vicious brain freeze.

I was walking back to my cabin when I ran into Big Bernice and a large group of girls. They must have been taking a victory lap. Bernice stopped and looked at me. I stood nervously, unsure of what was about to happen. Bernice opened her mouth and said, "I ain't never seen nobody eat so much ice cream so fast! You're crazier than a Boy Scout trying to sell cookies, and three times as stupid!"

I had no idea what she was talking about, but I smiled and said, "Yeah. I guess I was just trying to impress you girls, is all."

Bernice said that anyone as screwy as me couldn't be all bad, and invited me to go play kick the can with her and the girls. I agreed, and though I was surprised that their version of the game didn't involve dynamite, it still turned out to be kind of fun.

After that, taking part in camp activities turned out to be not so bad. I helped Big Bernice with her aim during archery practice, and she helped me make friendship bracelets out of macaroni. (Activities that don't include weapons aren't my strong suit.)

I even did OK in dance! (Dad's right—it does help your balance.)

Before I knew it, the weeks had flown by, and while there were no explosions . . . I was having a blast!

Our big trip to the Indian pyramids was the next morning . . .

That night we all sat around the campfire and sang songs. Miss Finkman thought I should try to sing a verse by myself. I must have eaten too many s'mores, because I agreed.

At least no one got mad at me this time.

All that hard work made me hungry again. I know the best way to make s'mores, which was taught to me by one of those Old West ghosts I told you about before. The secret is to have the marshmallow catch fire twice.

This was the first time I'd eaten s'mores with real human beings, not grumpy old-timey ghosts. It was . . . nice.

I was happy.

After the fire, I walked Breezy back to her cottage so we could go over her plans to find the lost Indian treasure. Even though camp had been fun, it was nice to think about dangerous situations again. I hadn't run for my life in nearly a month!

She had it all figured out. We'd wait for Miss Finkman to start snoring. (You could hear her from three counties away.)

Finkman's snores would provide ample cover for us to sneak off.

Once inside the temple, we'd follow Breezy's granddad's map to locate the lost treasure. It'd be easier than beating a werewolf zombie at Pokémon.

We said good night, and Breezy ran into her cabin. I was feeling pretty good about things, which is never a good sign.

Just then, I saw two shadows in the moonlight on the cabin wall.

It turns out that when the Doofuses had gotten wind that I was in summer camp, they had followed me there.

You'd think figuring out how to get dressed every morning would keep these morons occupied, but these two never cease to amaze me.

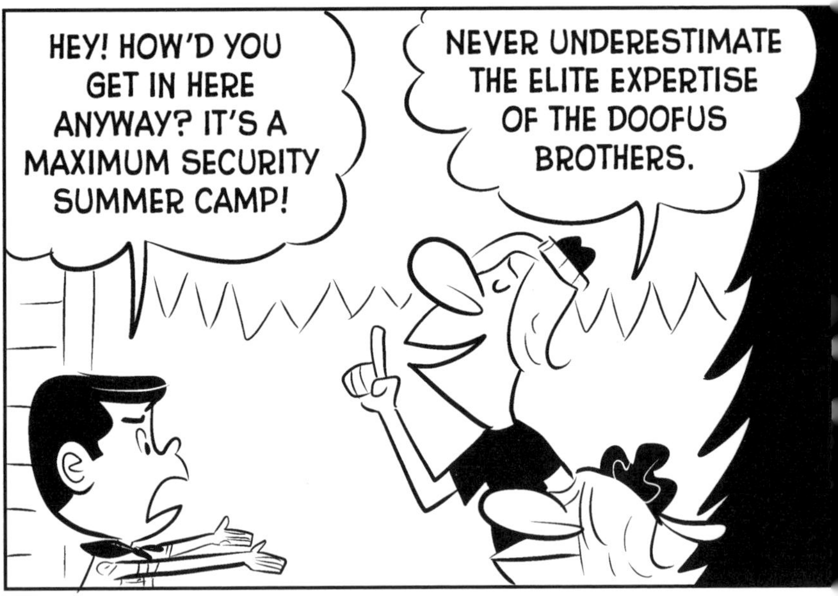
HEY! HOW'D YOU GET IN HERE ANYWAY? IT'S A MAXIMUM SECURITY SUMMER CAMP!
NEVER UNDERESTIMATE THE ELITE EXPERTISE OF THE DOOFUS BROTHERS.

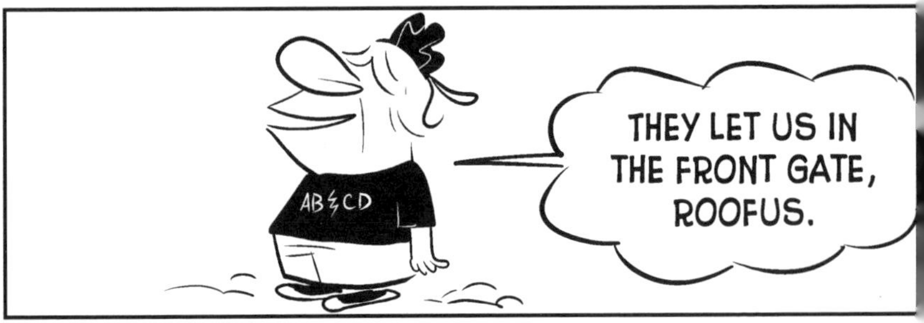
AB&CD
THEY LET US IN THE FRONT GATE, ROOFUS.

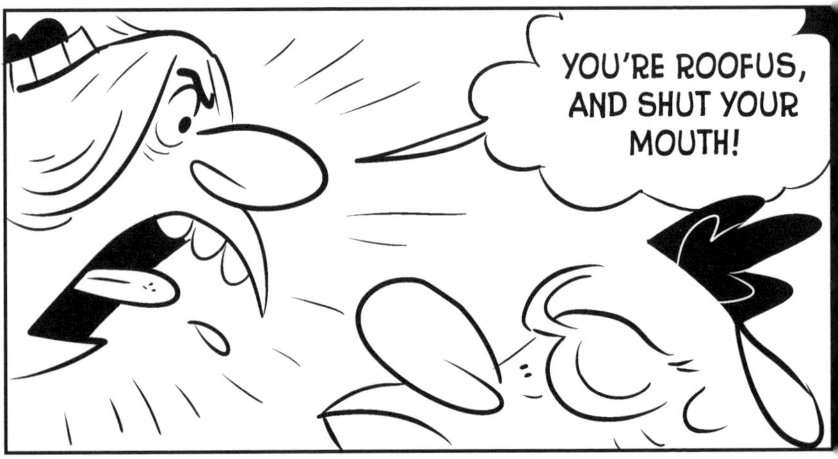
YOU'RE ROOFUS, AND SHUT YOUR MOUTH!

Once they'd followed me here, they'd done some snooping and heard about the trip to the Indian pyramid. Somehow, they pieced together the brainpower to figure out that the tomb was the likely hiding spot of the treasure. Maybe they'd been doing brain exercises or something.

So they sneakily took jobs as private tour guides to show the campers the pyramids. It was the perfect cover to follow me and snatch the treasure out from under my nose.

Except I wasn't here for treasure!

Except now I was!

THE DOOFUS BROTHERS DRIVE ME CRAZY!

Since they were guiding my camp mates through the Indian temple, they'd have complete control over us!

They said I might as well just cough up whatever treasure maps I had to make things easier. I played dumb.

I wasn't too worried. Even though they've caused a lot of problems for me over the years, they've only managed to steal treasure from me—never!

Although there was this one time—I almost hate to think about it . . .

Dad had entered me in a cross-desert camel race! First prize was 10,000 gold coins. Second prize was a year's worth of gourmet camel feed. Third prize was a toaster.

The weather was brutal. Temperatures reached 120 degrees at noon and dropped below freezing at night.

My camel didn't seem to care.

The Doofus Brothers had entered the race, too. They wanted to make sure I didn't win the gold. They didn't seem to mind if I got the camel food or the toaster.

They tried to drop rocks on me.

They tried to poison the water holes.

They tried to mess with my camel.

With all the time and effort they put into stopping me, they probably could have won the race themselves.

It was toward the end of the week, and most of the other racers had dropped out.

To keep my mind off the blistering heat, I tried to stay busy doing word ladders. Can you help me with this one?

WORD LADDER

BY CHANGING ONE LETTER IN EACH ROW, TURN DRY INTO HOT.

HINTS			
	D	R	Y
BETWEEN SUNRISE AND SUNSET			
DRIED GRASS			
HEAD COVERING			
	H	O	T

Solution on page 207

Finally, it was down to me and the Doofuses. I was almost to the finish line when I spotted something shiny in the shifting dunes.

I rode over and investigated. It was a gold cup! I dug in the sand underneath it and found a gold plate!

The Doofus Brothers showed up.

They shoved me aside and started digging.

I couldn't believe it! I'd found a whole city of gold, and then let the Doofus Brothers get the drop on me. I was too exhausted and dehydrated from the long desert trek to fight back! (Pro tip: Don't eat giant bags of Funyuns when racing through the blistering desert.) When I looked at the cup I was holding in my hand I noticed there was something written on the bottom.

The Doofuses were so blinded by the thought of finding a city filled with gold that they forgot all about me and the race.

I casually slipped away.

I easily won the race. And the Doofus Brothers?

CHAPTER 9

We left by bus for the Indian temple early the next morning. The Doofus Brothers sat up front, pretending to be tour guides, every once in a while giving me the stink eye. I tried to play sudoku to pass the time, but just the thought of those two idiots sitting there threw me off my game. After a long, tedious drive, we got off the bus and took canoes up a river to the temple. Evidently, ancient Indians didn't believe in building close to major highways.

The temple was huge! Even with the map, it was going to take a while to find the treasure. Hopefully, the ancient Indians didn't store it in the attic.

The Doofus Brothers were sticking to me like glue. Smelly, obnoxious glue.

We made camp near the river, and sat down for lunch. As the guides, the Doofus Brothers had brought Go-Gurts and Lunchables for everyone. They may be idiots, but they were actually kinda good guides!

I had to fill Breezy in on the true nature of the Doofuses.

YOU'VE GOT TO KEEP THAT MAP SAFE, BREEZY!

ROGER! IF THOSE TWO COME NEAR ME, THEY'RE GOING TO GET A BARBIE UP THE NOSE!

Now I had to figure out a way to sideline these two boobs.

Maybe I could fool the Doofuses into thinking the treasure was hidden *near* the temple instead of actually in it.

I'd leave a trail easy enough to follow and use one of the canoes we took to get there as a decoy. I'd push it downstream, they'd follow it, and by the time they realized it was a trick, it would be too late.

I sailed my decoy canoe for a bit, and then let it drift down the river while I swam in the opposite direction so I wouldn't leave any tracks.

I was heading back up the river when I saw the Doofuses take the bait. They hopped into a canoe and went after my decoy. I love it when a plan comes together.

As the smell of the Doofuses safely dwindled in the distance, I ran back to camp, with visions of an adventurous Doofus-free treasure hunt dancing in my head.

When I got back to camp, I saw everybody gathered around the radio. They looked worried.

And then one of the counselors who'd been swimming in the river ran into camp, yelling:

THE GUIDES ARE MISSING, AND SO ARE TWO CANOES! WE BETTER GET A REFUND!

If I didn't do something, the counselors were going to cancel the trip before it even got started! I had to stop that from happening if I wanted to help Breezy get that treasure! I needed to think of something fast!

The dire situation reminded me of the time Dad and I were exploring the deep, uncomfortably damp jungles of Gorilla Island.

The gorillas had captured a scientist who was doing research in the rain forest!

Dad sent me to try to find the missing scientist, Dr. Zane Goodyear. I guess he figured the great apes would be less threatened by a kid. Or he just wanted to watch the football game that day. Either way, it was me hacking my way through all that gorilla dander.

It turns out that one of the apes had stolen a bag of Dr. Zane's snack chips. I believe it was a bag of exploding-nacho-flavor Corn Bombs.

The ape tried one of the chips . . .
And loved it!

Instead of just eating all the chips and taking a nice nap, the gorilla immediately ran to the ape leader to show him the salty morsels that he'd discovered. Animals, right? They're totally crazy!

The apes went nuts for the Corn Bombs and devoured all of them! But it wasn't enough! Like ghost miners digging for gold, they just had to have more!

The gorillas kidnapped Dr. Zane Goodyear and demanded she cough up some more Corn Bombs! But she'd only brought a few bags, and they were history! (See my earlier pro tip about the necessity of bringing lots of salty snacks on most non-desert adventures.)

The gorillas thought the doctor was just stubbornly holding out on them, so they put her in jail!

Those dang dirty apes reminded me a lot of the Doofus Brothers. They even smelled fairly similar.

The tribe of gorillas was starting to get cranky! Their blood sugar levels must have been plummeting. If they didn't get more salt-filled, fat-laden chips soon, there was going to be serious trouble!

Luckily I had a bag of Corn Bombs in my backpack. While Funyuns are best for naval expeditions, Corn Bombs are ideal for jungle treks.

I needed to distribute the chips among the gorillas, or they were going to make me into a Corn Bomb! There were fifty-six Corn Bombs in the bag and eight gorillas. How many chips could I give to each gorilla?

I disguised myself as a gorilla god and . . .

The gorillas worshipped me like a hero! They thought I was some sort of Corn Bomb witch doctor with salty magical powers! I just hoped I had enough chips to distract them long enough.

I distributed the Corn Bombs evenly, and while the gorillas were eating I slipped away to free Dr. Zane Goodyear.

I had just made it into the jungle with the primate scientist when I heard the loud, angry crinkling of an empty Corn Bombs bag. The apes were fiending for more!

The race was on . . .

We ran like nobody's business, but the apes were right behind. You'd think all those Corn Bombs would have given them really wicked side stitches. Then Dr. Goodyear remembered that a supply boat was due to deliver a new shipment of Corn Bombs to a warehouse on the dock.

LET'S LEAD THEM TO THAT WAREHOUSE AND GET OFF THIS ROCK!

WHERE'S THE KEY TO THE WAREHOUSE?

I...I'M NOT SURE! MAYBE BACK IN THE TENT? OR IN MY PURSE? THE POCKETS OF MY OTHER SHORTS?

Without the key there was only one thing to do. I needed to bust down the door with my fists of steel.

I had learned from a kung fu master how to focus all your energy into your dukes and break like 100 blocks of ice.

FISTS OF STEEL!

The kung fu master was in the TV cartoon *Kung Fu Charlie*. But I think the lesson translated.

HE-YAAAH

KA-CRACK!

AUUUUUGH!

While I was teaching the lock who was boss, the gorillas found us! They could smell the chips in the warehouse, and it made them even grumpier. They charged us! But I was in so much pain, I didn't even care.

My screams of pain scared the gorillas. They probably thought I was turning into the Incredible Hulk. Also, one of the gorillas had managed to open the lock to the warehouse, thanks to me loosening it up for him with my mad kung fu skills.

Once the gorillas saw all the Corn Bombs, they forgot about us.

OH, WILL YOU LOOK AT THAT! THE KEY WAS IN MY FRONT POCKET ALL ALONG.

Anyway, the way I divided up the Corn Bombs between the gorillas that time gave me an idea how to divide up the campers among our decreased supply of boats. I told Miss Finkman that we could take the campers back to the bus in shifts, with one group staying behind while the other went up the river.

The storm clouds were rolling in. We had to move fast!

CHAPTER 10

With the hurricane bearing down on us, Breezy and I only had a short time to get to the pyramid to find the lost gold! How could we sneak away without the counselors wondering where we went? It was time to call on a friend for help!

Having friends is awesome!

I was hoping that this pyramid would be your basic open-plan tomb. No such luck. It turned out to be a huge maze filled with booby traps!

SPIKES FROM THE GROUND!

A GIANT CLEAVER THAT SPRANG FROM THE WALL!

The pyramid was a huge maze.

Finally, after having nearly every part of our bodies either nearly cut off, squashed, or covered in gross-smelling liquid fire, we came to a quiet room with a small fountain in the middle. The tinkling of the water echoed off the stones, and it smelled damp yet fresh, like plastic explosives that have fallen into a river.

THERE'S NOTHING ELSE IN HERE! COULD WE HAVE GONE THE WRONG WAY?

NO, I THINK WE FOUND WHAT WE'RE LOOKING FOR.

Breezy noticed that there were pictures on the wall of animals and numbers that we'd need to decode. It was a riddle that looked strangely familiar.

I'd seen something similar in my travels with Dad. We were on an adventure in outer space. By the way, I'm trusting that if anybody is reading this, they will keep it confidential.

There was a rogue alien artificial intelligence that was threatening to steal one of Earth's most precious resources . . . SUGAR!

The aliens were sending out sugar-stealing robots from a huge mother ship that was invisible to radar and was hiding on the other side of Saturn. Dad and I had some contacts in the area who tipped us off to the location of the alien base. It was my job to fly up there and make space safe for Earth sugar!

Now I don't know about you, but sugar is the main ingredient in all my favorite food and drinks. I wasn't about to sit by and let aliens take it to make gross alien candy or whatever.

Plus, I had enough gaming experience to send these robots back to their makers in itty-bitty pieces.

Once I blasted through the swarms of robot guards, it was a piece of cake to get into the mother ship.

I snuck in undetected and found the engine room.

I set the bombs, but then noticed something peculiar.

On the walls were markings . . . a sort of hieroglyphic. I took a photo with my iPad. My dad had gotten me a new one to replace the one that the abominable snowman stole.

After the bombs went off and destroyed the ship—which officially never existed—I showed Dad the photo.

He said that each symbol represented a letter. Once decoded, it read "Humans stink." The aliens had apparently encountered only teenagers.

So maybe these symbols represented letters, too. Maybe if you write down the first letters of the animals, numbers, and objects, you can decipher the code!

HELP ME AND BREEZY FIND THE CLUE!

We pushed the stone and suddenly the water in the fountain stopped and the floor started to rumble.

The fountain collapsed and turned into a staircase. Don't ask me what happened to all the water. All I know is that the stairs smelled worse than an abominable snowman's hot tub.

It didn't look like there were any booby traps. Aside from the smell, the stairs seemed more or less safe. We headed down them, breathing through our mouths.

The stairs led down, down, down. The Indians must have gotten a lot of exercise storing their treasure. Maybe they had a freight elevator hidden somewhere. After what seemed like stinky forever, we reached the bottom of the stairs and entered a huge room. The entrance was blocked by a huge barred gate. Behind the gate, in the far distance, we could make out the faint gleam of gold. Piles and piles of gold.

In front of the bars were two levers and another code for us to decipher.

We were all set to solve the code when I smelled a familiar stench and heard a familiar sound behind me.

It was the Doofus Brothers! Before I had a chance to react, they grabbed Breezy! I felt bad for her. Being that close to a Doofus is no picnic for your nostrils, and you pretty much have to burn any item of your clothing they touch.

I was beginning to wish I was back at camp, working on my dancing.

CHAPTER 11

Once again, the Doofus Brothers had me cornered. With Breezy in their hands, I couldn't risk making a move! I stood there and tried to control my rage.

While Breezy distracted the Doofuses with clever conversation, I looked at the two levers in front of the gate. My extensive knowledge of ancient booby traps led me to believe that one opened the gate and the other led to sticky, unpleasant injury or death.

You have to hand it to these ancient cultures. They sure knew how to mess with treasure hunters.

I looked at the symbols on the wall, thinking about all I knew about hieroglyphics, codes, ancient cultures, and spicy soft tacos. (I was pretty hungry.) I think I knew which lever to pull.

But if I pulled the correct lever, the Doofuses would get the treasure. And that was more than I could stand! I had to get them to pull the wrong lever somehow.

And treasure or no treasure, I had to get me and Breezy out of here alive!

The last time I was in a jam this serious, I was in the jungle, getting squeezed by a giant anaconda!

I had been exploring in the rain forest, innocently looking for lost civilizations, when this huge snake dropped out of a tree and right onto my head! Before I knew it, he was squeezing me but good! (If I'd had that machete that Dad keeps promising me, this wouldn't have been a problem. But a Junior Scout knife ain't much good against a giant snake.)

The anaconda was really enjoying my predicament.

This snake had a huge ego. I couldn't believe I had to spend my last moments listening to this windbag. It was then that I thought of something. This snake's weakness was his inflated opinion of himself.

The snake thought about it. I could tell that my psychological tricks were working. Arrogant jerks are always insecure deep down.

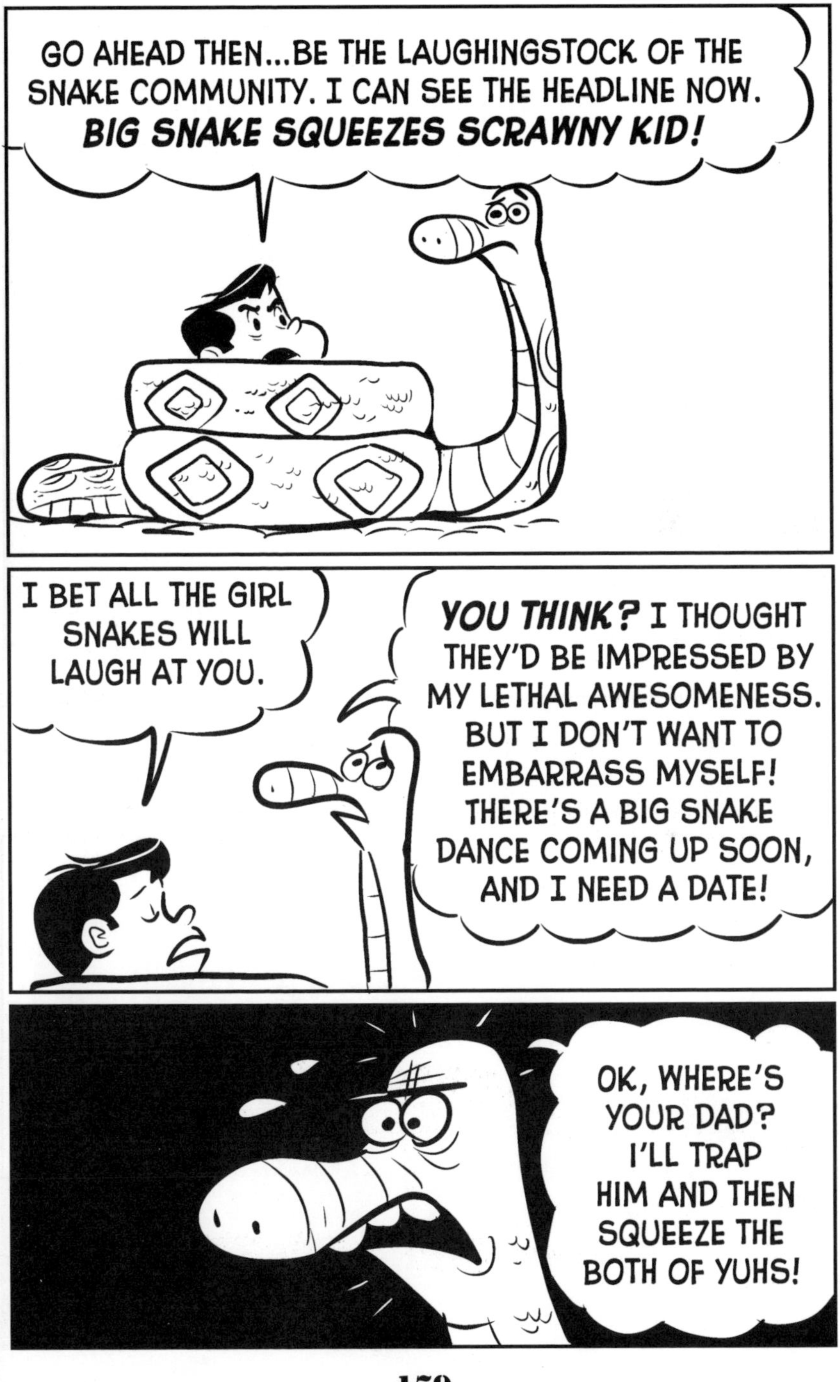
GO AHEAD THEN...BE THE LAUGHINGSTOCK OF THE SNAKE COMMUNITY. I CAN SEE THE HEADLINE NOW. *BIG SNAKE SQUEEZES SCRAWNY KID!*
I BET ALL THE GIRL SNAKES WILL LAUGH AT YOU.
YOU THINK? I THOUGHT THEY'D BE IMPRESSED BY MY LETHAL AWESOMENESS. BUT I DON'T WANT TO EMBARRASS MYSELF! THERE'S A BIG SNAKE DANCE COMING UP SOON, AND I NEED A DATE!
OK, WHERE'S YOUR DAD? I'LL TRAP HIM AND THEN SQUEEZE THE BOTH OF YUHS!

I told him that he'd never be able to sneak up on my dad. He wasn't a good enough anaconda to trap an expert warrior like him.

I told him that Dad has a collection of snakeskin boots that he makes from the snakes that have tried to kill him. He doesn't like wearing them because snakeskin is more uncomfortable than off-brand sneakers, but he does so he can remember all the dumb snakes that tried to kill him and have a good laugh.

The snake's blood got colder and colder. Which is pretty impressive, because snakes are already cold-blooded animals. If he wasn't careful, he was going to be a snake pop!

You could see the snake running through his options in his tiny snake brain.

It worked like a charm.

But could I convince the Doofus Brothers to pick the wrong lever to open the gate to the treasure? Could Breezy and I escape before the booby trap went off? The floor was wet. What had happened to all the water in the fountain? Where had it gone? I looked around and noticed a big drain in the floor. The water had been siphoned out into the river outside the temple!

I noticed other big drains on the wall. But why would anyone need drains on a wall, unless maybe you were a really violent sneezer? Then it hit me: They weren't drains, they were pipes!

I bet that pulling the wrong lever would open the pipes and let water from the river flood into the room, filling it completely!

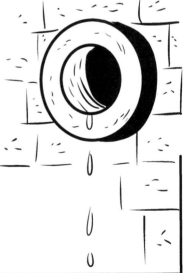

If we could make it to the stairs before the water got to us, we'd have a chance. I'd managed to figure out what the hieroglyphics on the wall said: "WARNING: Right Lever for Booby Trap Only. Pull at Your Own Risk!" I had to trick the Doofuses into pulling the lever on the right. Our lives depended on it!

OK, RUNTWIRE! YOU'VE GOT US THIS FAR THROUGH THE BOOBY TRAPS! NOW OPEN THE GATE TO THE TREASURE!

Then I rolled my eyes like I was saying, "Ha-ha, dummy."

There was a long pause. It always takes the Doofuses a while to form a thought.

IT'S THE LEFT ONE. NOW LEAVE US ALONE.

HEAR THAT, ROOFUS? THE LEFT ONE. WE'RE RICH!

I BLEW IT.

FINALLY, AFTER ALL THESE YEARS OF ALMOST BEATING HAYWIRE, WE'RE GOING TO FINALLY DO IT! I CAN'T BELIEVE IT!

YOU'RE RIGHT. THAT WAS *TOO* EASY.

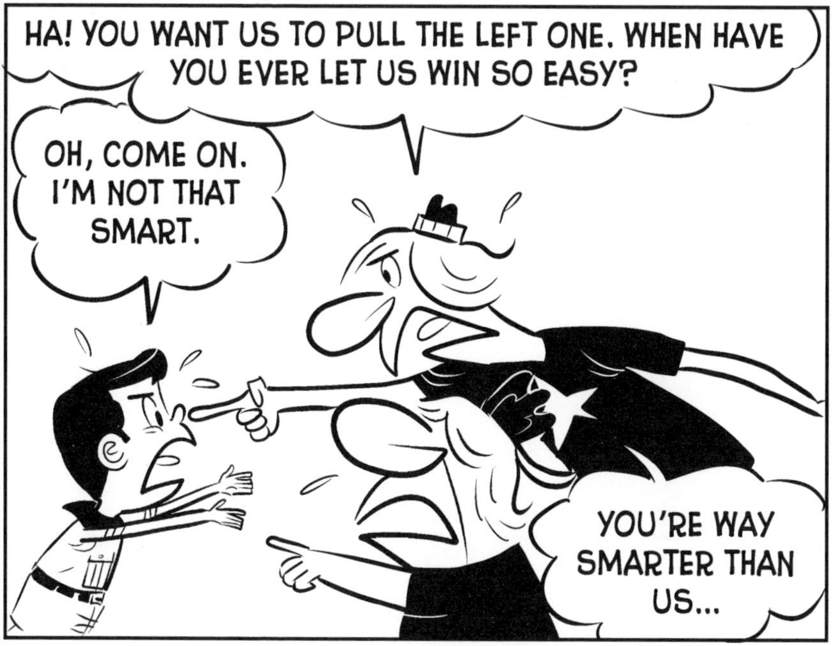
HA! YOU WANT US TO PULL THE LEFT ONE. WHEN HAVE YOU EVER LET US WIN SO EASY?
OH, COME ON. I'M NOT THAT SMART.
YOU'RE WAY SMARTER THAN US...

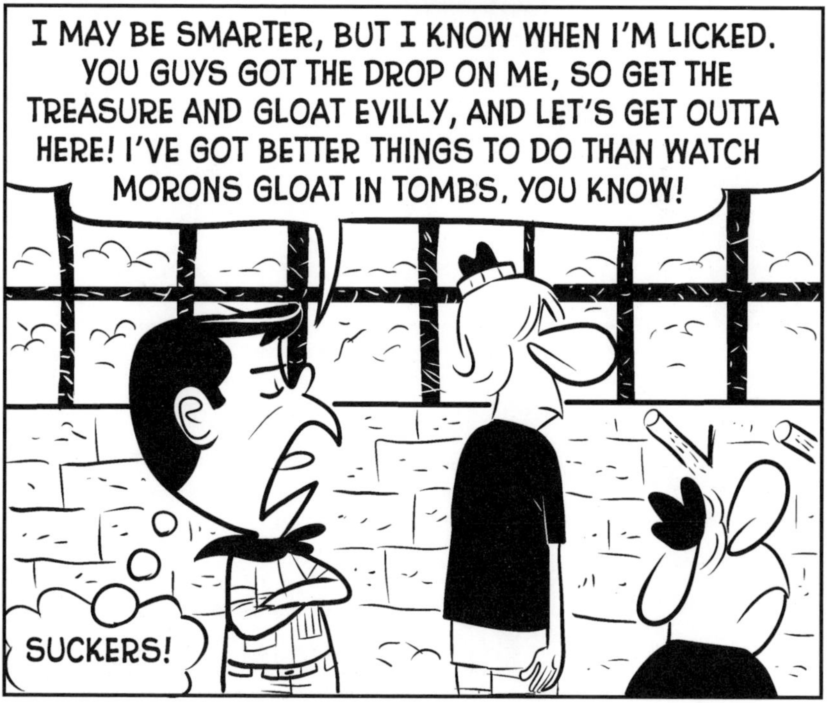
I MAY BE SMARTER, BUT I KNOW WHEN I'M LICKED. YOU GUYS GOT THE DROP ON ME, SO GET THE TREASURE AND GLOAT EVILLY, AND LET'S GET OUTTA HERE! I'VE GOT BETTER THINGS TO DO THAN WATCH MORONS GLOAT IN TOMBS, YOU KNOW!
SUCKERS!

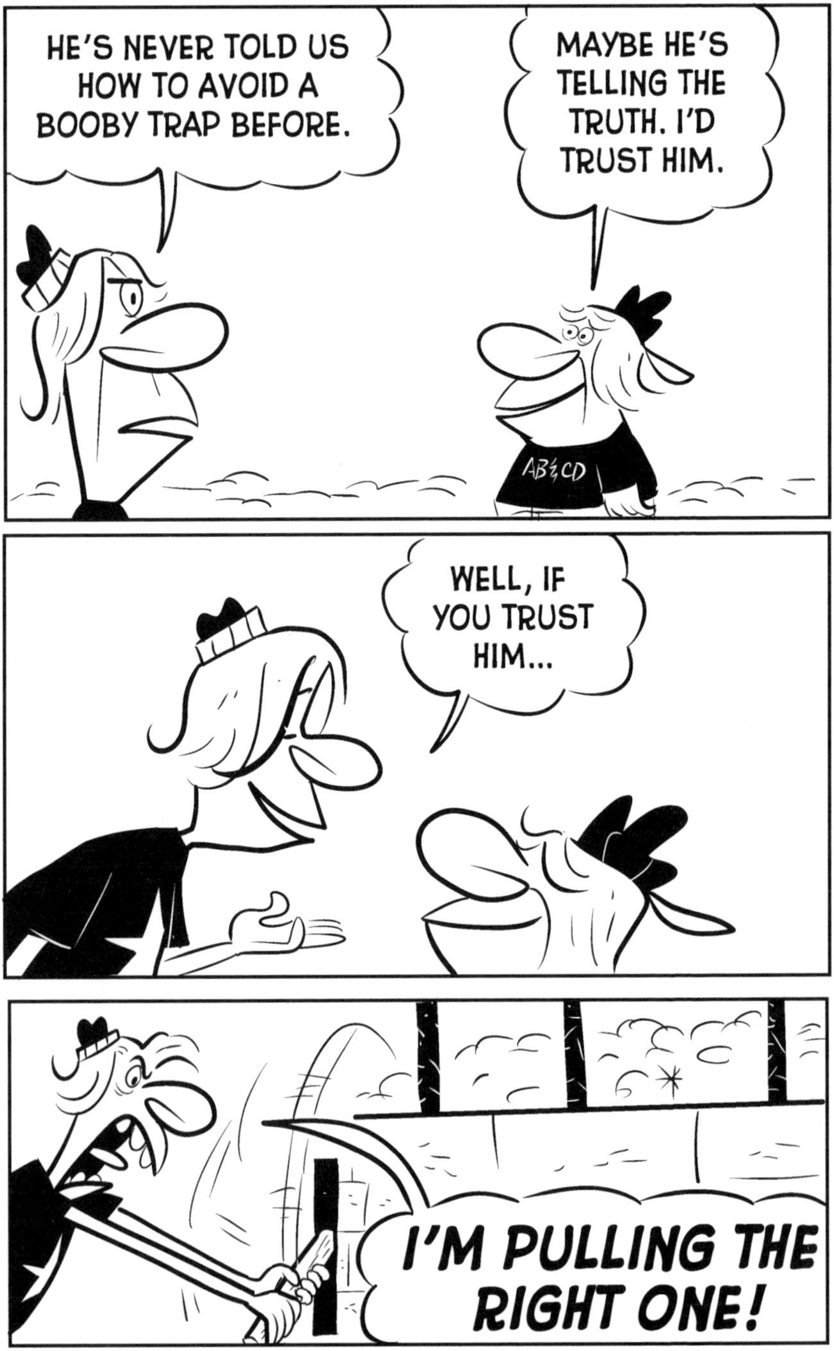
HE'S NEVER TOLD US HOW TO AVOID A BOOBY TRAP BEFORE.
MAYBE HE'S TELLING THE TRUTH. I'D TRUST HIM.
AB¾CD
WELL, IF YOU TRUST HIM...
I'M PULLING THE RIGHT ONE!

Just as Roofus pulled the lever to activate the booby trap, I told Breezy to run toward the stairs!

I was right behind her.

The water filled up the room like it was a kiddie pool! We barely made it to the stairs before the water pushed us the rest of the way up. It was like surfing but without a board. It was pretty fun!

We fell on our butts, and when we looked back, the fountain was back in business.

As for the Doofus Brothers, the water shot up through the pyramid like a geyser, taking them along with it.

They landed miles upriver. To this day, they're afraid of water fountains.

CHAPTER 12

By the time we got out of the pyramid, the sky was turning a distinctly threatening shade of purple. The hurricane! In our excitement with the treasure and then the Doofuses, we'd forgotten about it!

As we thought about what to do, the first raindrops began to fall. We had to hurry! We ran back to the river where we met up with Big Bernice and the remaining campers. Luckily, Miss Finkman hadn't returned with the canoes yet.

By the time Finkman did get back, the storm was really settling in. We didn't have time to get all the way back to camp; we rowed upriver to take shelter in some nearby caves.

We barely made it to shelter before the full force of the hurricane bashed down upon us. The wind howled like an abominable snowman who'd just accidentally erased his Minecraft game. The rain pelted down like an endless hail of hollow-point bullets. It was unbelievable! I'd been in a lot of dangerous situations before, but never had I felt so . . . powerless. You can't outsmart, outpunch, or escape a storm. You just have to sit there and wait until it's over. As this terrifying thought crept through my bones, I looked at Miss Finkman and the other campers. They were scared, too! And suddenly, seeing that I had company, I didn't feel so bad.

From then on, things got better. We spent the night playing games, telling stories, and having fun. Breezy told a story about her first day of kindergarten that made one of my adventures sound tame, and Big Bernice told a story about her older brother that made the abominable snowman sound like Frosty.

And y'know, it's funny, but just listening and talking to the other kids made things seem less scary. The night even passed kind of quickly.

The next morning, the sky cleared, the sun came out, and everything was bright and clean. Plus, the storm had knocked a bunch of trees down, which was pretty cool.

We headed back to Pink PowderPuff Summer Camp.

Later on we told everyone about the lost treasure. And not only was Breezy able to give the credit of the discovery to her grandpa, she gave him somthing else too:

Breezy's grandpa was ecstatic! Then the man went full-blown lunatic!

Here's a picture that was in the newspaper.

He was honored and Breezy was really happy. I could tell that after all that I had done for her, she thought I was pretty hot stuff.

Now that everything was settled and we were back at camp, we were going to go fishing and play hoops. Big Bernice was on my team . . . win!

I was just leaving my cottage when, of all people, my dad showed up.

That did sound like fun, but I was also having a blast at camp.

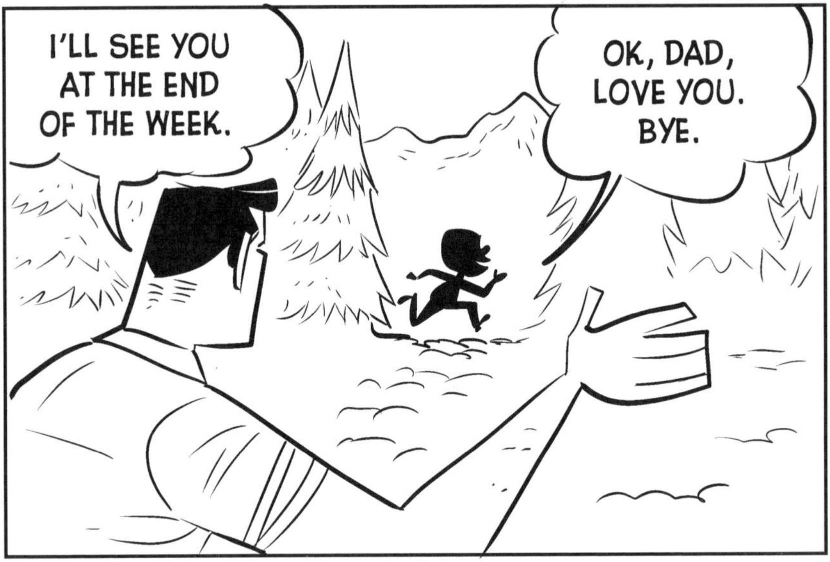
I'LL SEE YOU AT THE END OF THE WEEK.
OK, DAD, LOVE YOU. BYE.

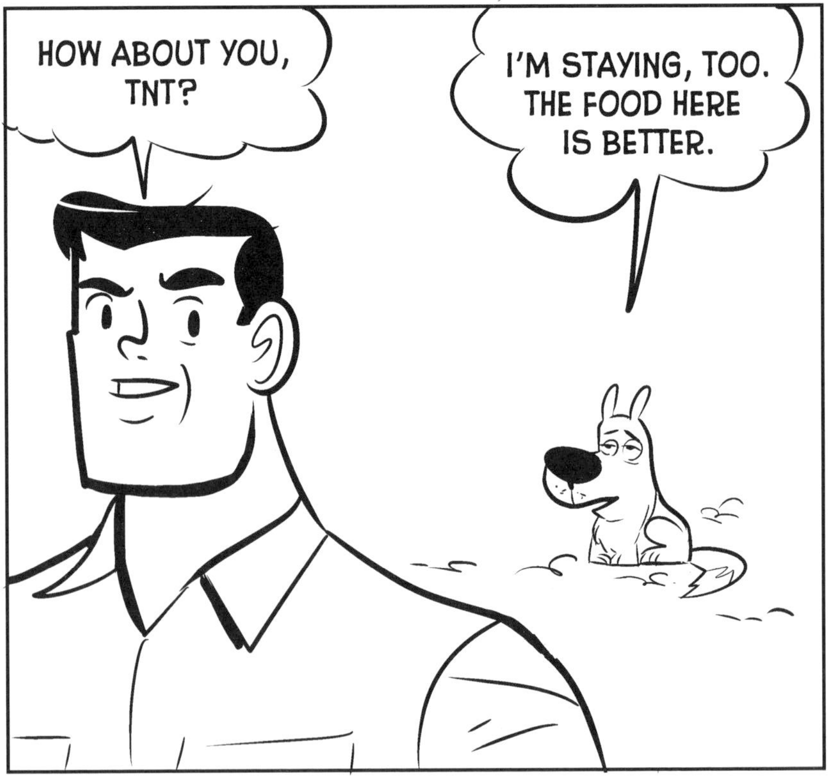
HOW ABOUT YOU, TNT?
I'M STAYING, TOO. THE FOOD HERE IS BETTER.

And so that was the great adventure of Pink PowderPuff Summer Camp.

Oh, one more thing. In case you ever go there and want to escape—which would be crazy, but still—I learned this little nugget of wisdom.

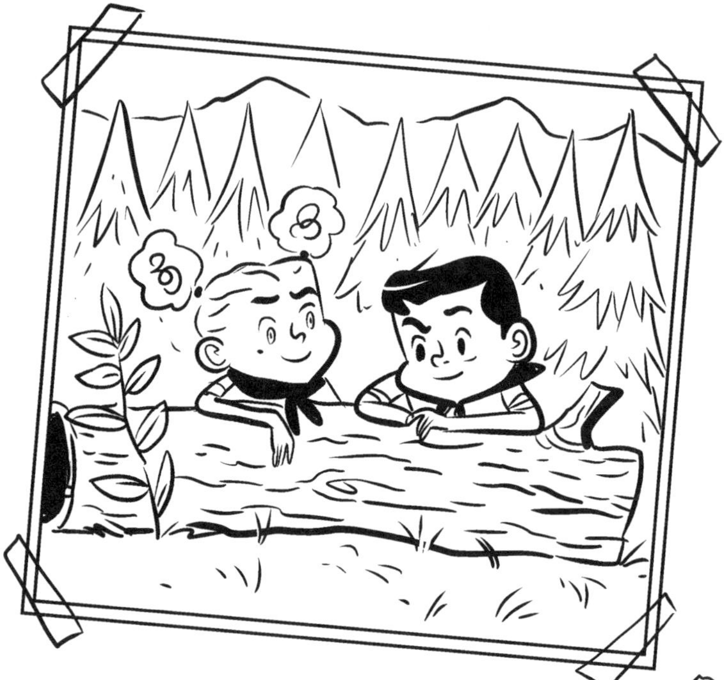

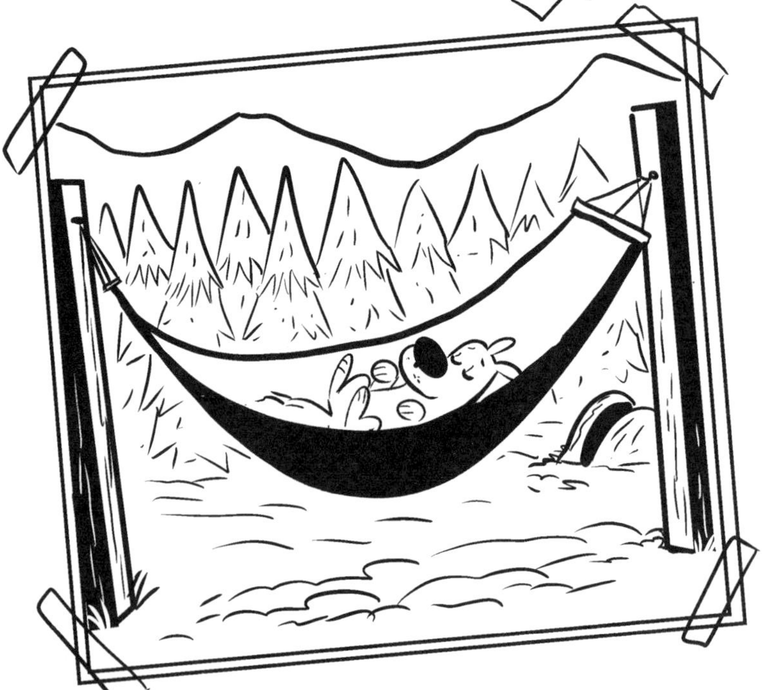

Now, even when I'm helping my dad escape from
mole-people who live at the center of the Earth or fin
King Solomon's mines, I still look forward to going to Pink
PowderPuff Summer Camp more than anything. Breezy
even sends me tons of letters; she misses me so much:

Dear Rip,

I'm glad you were able to escape the mole-people's clutches on your own, 'cuz my grandpa wasn't going to give them the ransom they asked for. Next time you're in trouble, leave me out of it! And you don't need to send me so many letters either. See you at camp next year. If you've learned not to clomp all over my feet by then, maybe I'll dance with you, but probably not.

See ya, Breezy.

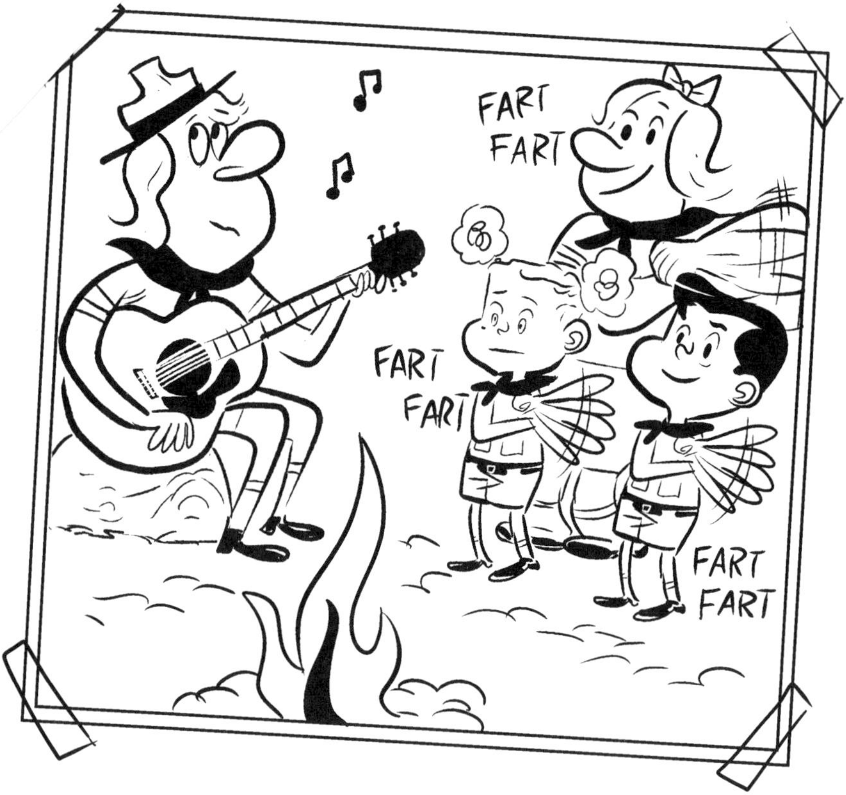
FART
FART
FART
FART
FART
FART

THE END

MORE TO EXPLORE

FUN FACTS ABOUT THE PLACES RIP AND TNT VISIT DURING THEIR MANY ADVENTURES!

My adventure going up against the abominable snowman or yeti has probably got you wondering if these creatures actually exist . . . and whether they have grown tired of playing on my iPad yet.

Well here's what I "dug up." (That's a little adventurer pun for you.)

The first report of a strange apelike creature living in the Himalayan region of Nepal and Tibet (in Asia) dates back to 1832, when climber B.H. Hodgson witnessed a tall beast covered in hair walking on two feet.

The locals who claim to have seen the yeti say that the beast comes in two different types: *dzu-teh*, which is 7 to 8 feet tall, and *meh-teh*, which is only 5 to 6 feet tall. But most authorities agree that the yeti is tall, with both human and apelike characteristics, and probably doesn't smell very good.

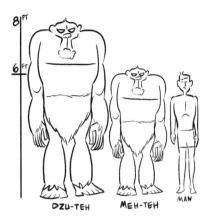

So far, hard proof of the yeti's existence hasn't actually materialized, but that doesn't mean it's not real. It'd probably get out more if it wasn't so addicted to Minecraft.

As for the curse of the mummy, that's a different story. Mummies are definitely real—you can see them in many museums if you don't mind getting grossed out—but their ability to curse, not so much.

Some people think the legend of a mummy's curse comes from the fact that in the old days, grave robbers often became ill. (Grave robbers were after the precious items that were buried with important people.) But that was because dead bodies can carry germs that are dangerous to living people.

In 1827, Jane C. Loudon wrote a fantasy novel called *The Mummy!* in which an angry mummy comes back to life in search of revenge.

There is no evidence that the ancient Egyptians believed that mummies were cursed. At least, that's what the mummies want you to think . . .

MWA-HA-HA-HA-HAAAA!

Page 18:

Page 33: The camper's age is 7.

Page 43: The fake is number 3 with a broken fang.

Page 61:
YOU CAN LOOK
BUT DON'T TOUCH OR ELSE
I CURSE YOU!

Page 80: ENTER AT YOUR OWN RISK

Page 91:
1 DUCK
2 HORSE
3 DONKEY

Page 115:

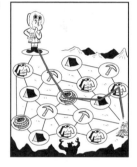

Page 137:
DRY
DAY
HAY
HAT
HOT

Page 160:

Page 167:
PUSH THE
STONE ON THE
FOUNTAIN

Li'l Rip Haywire Adventures: Escape from Camp Cooties copyright © 2016 by Dan Thompson. All rights reserved.
Printed in China. No part of this book may be used or reproduced in any manner whatsoever without written
permission except in the case of reprints in the context of reviews.

Andrews McMeel Publishing
a division of Andrews McMeel Universal
1130 Walnut Street, Kansas City, Missouri 64106

www.andrewsmcmeel.com

16 17 18 19 20 SDB 10 9 8 7 6 5 4 3 2 1

ISBN: 978-1-4494-7051-7

Library of Congress Control Number: 2015943470

Made by: Shenzhen Donnelley Printing Company Ltd.
Address and location of manufacturer: No. 47, Wuhe Nan Road, Bantian Ind. Zone, Shenzhen China, 518129
1st Printing - 12/7/15

ATTENTION: SCHOOLS AND BUSINESSES

Andrews McMeel books are available at quantity discounts with bulk purchase for educational, business, or sales
promotional use. For information, please e-mail the Andrews McMeel Publishing Special Sales Department:
specialsales@amuniversal.com.